DAPHNE CLAIR

marriage under fire

Harlequin Books

TORONTO • NEW YORK • LONDON
AMSTERDAM • PARIS • SYDNEY • HAMBURG
STOCKHOLM • ATHENS • TOKYO • MILAN

Harlequin Presents first edition May 1984
ISBN 0-373-10687-4

Original hardcover edition published in 1983
by Mills & Boon Limited

Books by Daphne Clair

HARLEQUIN PRESENTS

HARLEQUIN ROMANCES

These books may be available at your local bookseller.

For a free catalog listing all titles currently available,
send your name and address to:

Harlequin Reader Service
P.O. Box 52040, Phoenix, AZ 85072-2040
Canadian address: Stratford, Ontario N5A 6W2

"Shut up!" he snarled. "You asked for this."

He silenced her with a bruising kiss on her mouth, and then she was tossed on the bed, gasping, "Jason, *don't*!"

"I told you to be quiet," he muttered, throwing off his robe, and one hand pushed her back on the pillows as he came down beside her, sliding his hand from her shoulder to the crook of her elbow and holding her still.

"Please," she panted, trying to stave him off with one hand on his chest.

"Don't ask me to be gentle," he said harshly, his eyes glittering. "I don't feel gentle. I don't feel kind. I want to make love to you so thoroughly that you'll cry for mercy. I want to imprint myself on you so deeply that you won't even remember his name. I *won't* have you confusing me with *him*. I *won't*—be gentle!"

CHAPTER ONE

CATHERINE pushed a strand of fair hair from her eyes, but the brisk wind whipped it against her damp lashes again, so that she had to keep her hand on it as she stood watching the plane take off. The viewing platform was exposed and cold, making her shiver as she strained to see if Michael and Jenny were waving to her from behind one of the increasingly distant porthole windows.

They seemed so young to be flying off alone across the Tasman ... Jenny had looked apprehensive, biting her lip to stop it from trembling, and even Michael, at six a year older than his sister, had surreptitiously wiped a small tear away on the sleeve of his new jacket.

She couldn't see them at all, but she waved vigorously anyway, fixing a smile on her face although they would be too far away by now to see it. The plane taxied along the runway, turned, and seemed to pause for an age before it began to trundle its impossible weight along with gathering speed until it lifted off gracefully into the cloud-spattered morning and rose swiftly over the sparkling water of the Manukau.

The stewardesses would look after the children very well, the airline was noted for its special care, providing games and puzzles and plenty of distraction for them. They would be met at Sydney by their grandparents, and have a thoroughly good time for the next two months ...

'My parents will spoil them rotten,' Jason had assured her. 'We'll have our hands full when they

5

get back. But it will be good for them. Teach them a bit of independence. They'll love it!'

But Catherine had been unable to hide her unease, and later he had said impatiently, 'Well, if you're so worried, why don't you go with them? The invitation was open to you, too.'

She had looked at him with sudden curiosity. He was putting on his tie, dressing for work. She could see the back of his dark, sleek head, and his mirrored face, a faint frown between the straight brows echoed in the slight tightness about his firm mouth. He looked up and met her eyes in the mirror, his dark grey and enigmatic, and hers jade green flecked with gold, questioning and rather uncertain.

'Wouldn't you mind?' she asked him.

She was sitting up in their bed, her hair falling over her shoulders, the strap of a gold satin nightdress he had bought her slipping down one arm. For a moment a spark lit his eyes as they slithered over her, and her heartbeat quickened a little. Then he turned away from her and caught up his jacket to shrug it on. 'I guess I'd survive—somehow,' he said indifferently. He came over to her and touched his lips briefly to her cheek, patted the other one and said, 'Come on, lazybones. The kids will be late for school.'

As he left, Catherine got up, sighing with an unaccountable feeling of depression. She had learned early in their marriage that Jason never ate breakfast. He would get himself a glass of juice from the refrigerator, have a quick look at the headlines in the paper, scan the business pages and go. At first when he said to her, 'Stay there—you might as well,' and pressed her back on to the pillows of the bed, she had ignored him and accompanied him into the kitchen. But she soon found that he was serious about not wanting breakfast, and also that he liked some time alone with the paper. Once she had teased him about how quickly their married life had settled into the conventional rut at breakfast time, and he gave a faint, absent-minded smile and said, 'I told you not to get up.'

Of course, once the children came she was not able to stay in bed if she had wanted to. Frequently she was up before Jason, and as the children reached school age he had got accustomed to sharing the breakfast table with them and dropping them off at school on his way to work. Jenny had turned five and started school in the second term, and Catherine had found herself strangely at a loose end. The house seemed very empty all day, with no children in it until Jenny and Michael returned from school.

A friend had inveigled her into attending a daytime art class for some weeks, but although she had quite enjoyed the activity, she was no artist, and when they progressed beyond sketching and watercolours to oils, she watched the others in the class turning out presentable landscapes and dashing abstracts, surveyed her own mud-coloured, wooden-looking efforts, and ruefully decided to give it up.

'I'll never be an artist,' she confessed to Jason, when he queried her decision.

'You don't need to be. It would have made an interesting hobby for you. I thought you enjoyed it.'

Catherine shrugged. 'I did, for a while. Jason . . . supposing I got a job, now that the children are at school . . .?'

'A job? What for?'

'Well—for something to do.'

'Not a good idea,' he said dryly.

'I don't see why not.'

'For one thing, you could only work part-time—unless you were thinking of palming Michael and Jenny off on someone else after school. Also, there's a shortage of jobs at the moment and a lot of people don't take kindly to the idea of married women whose husbands earn adequate salaries taking jobs to relieve their boredom——'

'I don't think that's a valid argument. Women have as much right to work as men, married or not! Why shouldn't a woman pursue a career?'

'What career were you thinking of?'

'I—I don't know.' She had been training to be a teacher before she married Jason, but she had not finished the course, and now, apparently, there was a surplus of teachers anyway. New Zealand's birthrate had plummeted and too many teachers were scrambling for too few jobs.

'Well, you would be just filling in time, wouldn't you? Taking a job you don't need which could be filled by someone who really does need it.'

'I suppose so,' she admitted.

'What about those committees that you're on?' he said. 'The hospital whatsit and the Plunket Society?'

'I resigned from the Plunket committee,' she reminded him. 'Now that the children aren't babies any more, I've lost interest.'

'You seem to lose interest in things rather often.'

'That isn't fair! I felt I should pull my weight as long as I was using the services of the Plunket nurse, but I don't *enjoy* committee work. I was glad to give it up.'

'Are you going to give up the hospital one, too?'

'No, I don't think so. I don't like the meetings

much, there's a lot of time wasted, but they do some useful work, and visiting the wards is something that seems worthwhile to me.'

'Maybe that's something you should give up,' he suggested abruptly.

'*Why?*'

'Do you think I don't notice that it upsets you? Did you have to volunteer for the children's wards?'

'I'd be more upset if I thought no one was visiting them. It isn't easy finding volunteers. It isn't always upsetting. Sometimes it's fun.'

'Some fun, when you come home and indulge in a crying bout!'

'It only happened once,' Catherine said huskily. She had stopped crying by the time Jason got home; she had been cooking the dinner, while Michael and Jenny argued over a game at the table. He had looked at her sharply and asked, 'What's the matter?'

'Nothing. I was at the hospital this afternoon.'

'And——?'

She looked at the children and shook her head. 'Sometimes it's a bit harrowing,' she said. 'Jenny—Michael! Put that away now and set the table for me, please.'

The children protested and she insisted, and Jason stood aside, then shrugged and made for their room to put away his jacket as Catherine returned her attention to the sauce she was stirring on the stove. Jason had had a meeting to go to that evening, and the next day he appeared to have forgotten about the incident.

But now, weeks later, he said, 'What was it about?'

'I got fond of a child,' she said baldly. 'He died.'

Several seconds ticked by. Catherine was

looking down at her hands, and Jason hadn't moved. Then he said, 'I see. Why didn't you tell me?'

'In front of the children?'

'Later—the next day!'

'You didn't ask, the next day.'

'I didn't realise that it was anything that shattering. Catherine——'

They were interrupted then by Michael, demanding his father's help to get his ball down off the roof where he had accidentally thrown it. The subject had not arisen again.

Catherine had not taken a job, but she had become involved in an ambitious project of the hospital committee to stage a Christmas pantomime at the hospital. She was given one of the leading parts as the Good Fairy, and had also written much of the script, a mixture of fairytale glamour for the children and witty remarks which would also entertain the adults in the audience. She had something of a flair for entertaining writing, remarked on by her friends who received her letters, and her bedtime stories were as often made up from her own imagination as they were read from Michael's and Jenny's books.

It was the pantomime that prevented her from accompanying the children on their seven weeks' visit to their grandparents in Australia. The rehearsals would continue until Christmas, and the first performance was scheduled for Boxing Day, with a repeat a week later for geriatric patients. Some of the long-term mobile patients were among the performers, including a number of children, but the main parts were carried by the committee members.

Catherine had not really wanted to go to Australia, but she would miss the children, and

couldn't help feeling stupidly anxious in case
something happened to the plane, or through some
mix-up Jason's parents failed to meet it. They
might be travel-sick or homesick, or one of them
might have an accident . . .

It was all nonsense, of course, and she voiced
only half of these fears to Jason, knowing she was
fussing for no reason. Of course she trusted his
parents to care for the children. They loved their
only two grandchildren devotedly. Usually they
flew from Australia for Christmas to be with them,
but this year was different. Winston Clyde, who
had taken his family from New Zealand to
Australia for business reasons when Jason was
fifteen, had retired and moved to a new home on
the famous Gold Coast. He wanted to give his
grandchildren the holiday of their lives. The whole
family had been invited, but Catherine knew that
Jason had not really been expected to accept the
invitation. Her own refusal was probably half
expected, too. She and her parents-in-law got on
well enough in a superficial way, but she had never
been truly at ease with Winston's rather pugnaci-
ous drive for success in everything, or Althea's
cool graciousness. Both of them unbent considerably with the children, but Catherine had always
felt that they had thought her too young, too
gauche and altogether lacking in the things needed
for the wife of a successful businessman when she
had married Jason. And although over the last
eight years she had grown a veneer of sophistication and poise, it always seemed to peel away in
their presence, leaving her the slightly awkward
and tongue-tied young girl she had been at their
first meeting.

'She's just a teenager!' Althea had exclaimed in
surprise, and Catherine had seen the quick,

scowlingly questioning look that Winston had shot
at his son. Because Jason was touching thirty, and
already established on the ladder of success in the
finance company he worked for. She had seen the
tightening of his mouth and the flush staining the
taut flesh over his cheekbones as he met his
father's gaze with steady, defiant eyes, and with an
unaccustomed rush of protectiveness towards him,
she had said quickly, 'I'm older than I look.'

'Not more than twenty, I'll be bound,' Winston
had said shrewdly, with a short, hard laugh.

Jason moved, putting his arm about Catherine's
shoulders, saying, 'She's eighteen.' And at the
same time, she said, 'I'm nineteen——'

Jason slanted a wry grin at her, and she added,
'——nearly.'

Jason looked resigned. She had made herself
look foolish and younger than ever, of course. She
wasn't making a good impression.

She still felt that she never had made a good
impression on Jason's parents. She didn't know
anything about the business world that Winston
inhabited—and that Jason did, too—and she
didn't share Althea's passion for bridge, or her
interest in antiques. Once the children came it was
a little easier, though she found Althea's constant
smoothly given advice a little hard to take. All the
same, she was very glad that while Michael and
Jenny were still babies, Jason had taken a new and
important executive job in New Zealand and
moved them all across the Tasman. Her own
father had died some years ago, and her mother
had married again and was living in Western
Australia. Catherine hardly ever saw her after her
own marriage, although they kept faithfully in
touch by letter.

Her mother had been doubtful about her

marrying Jason, at first, but she had soon come round after she met him. Jason was obviously good husband material. He had looks and brains and a solid career in finance, and a quietly confident manner that would have reassured any anxious mother. He told her that he realised that Catherine was young to be marrying a man of his age, but that he promised she would be well looked after. And Catherine's mother had seen the way he looked at her daughter, and given her blessing.

'Provided it's what Catherine wants,' she had added. And Jason had smiled at Catherine, his eyes dark and almost hypnotic.

'Is it what you want, Catherine?' he asked her softly.

For just a moment she hesitated, her hand in his, until she felt the tightening of his fingers, sending a signal of warm excitement into her body. He had dazzled her from the start, with his unexpected interest in her, his assurance, and eventually with the restrained passion of his kisses. Now he had only to touch her and she felt herself ready to burst into flame.

She said, 'Yes. It's what I want.'

She had got what she wanted—what he had wanted—because sometimes she wondered, now, if she had ever made a decision, herself, that she really wanted to marry Jason. She had been so young, and he was the first real man who had crossed her path. She had known boys before that, boys who touched her heart lightly and passed on, who had never even tried very hard to drag her into the depths of real passion. But Jason was different. She had known from the start Jason wasn't interested in playing light love games. Even when they first met, at a party, both of them there with someone else, and he had asked how to contact her, she had hesitated.

'Are you going steady or something?' he asked her, amused.

Catherine shook her head.

'Well, then?' He stood before her, a notebook and pencil in his hand, waiting. They had been talking, laughing together, getting on simply fine until he demanded her telephone number. 'Don't be coy,' he said. 'I can get it from our hostess, anyway. I'll find you.'

It sounded almost like a threat, and she searched his eyes with hers wide and a little wary. His face softened a little. He said quietly, 'Don't look like that. I don't intend to ravish you, fair maiden.'

The ridiculous appellation, the thread of humour in his voice, made her giggle and capitulate. He took down the number, said, 'Right, you'll be hearing from me,' and departed to pay some attention to his own partner.

Catherine had wondered if she would, or if it was a whim which he would forget, and after three weeks had passed, she had decided that he had indeed forgotten all about her. But then he had phoned, asked her out to dinner, and followed it with more invitations. She had never asked him why he let so much time elapse before contacting her, but sometimes had an uneasy suspicion that it had been a purposeful ploy to keep her in suspense and make her more eager to go out with him.

He had wined and dined her, and made her laugh. He had an ironic sense of humour that she enjoyed, and she even brought a crack of laughter from him on occasion, because she had a quick mind, a sense of the ridiculous, and an ability to spin words which he encouraged. She loved to dance, and he took her dancing at places her younger escorts could never have afforded. He even bought her flowers. When he kissed her, he did it with a light expertise that promised more, until the day came when she felt her wary reserve with him melt away, and kissed him back with her arms about his neck.

He pulled back from her, looking down at her face, muttered. 'I've been waiting for that,' and kissed her again.

This time it was quite different. Her mouth parted under a gentle, insistent assault, and Jason's hand possessed her breast, while his other arm curved her body closely to the contours of his. They seemed locked together for an eternity in an agony of sensation, and she discovered that she loved the warmth, the unbelievable intimacy of his mouth on hers, tasting, exploring, taking her over.

When he gradually eased his hold she was shaking and gasping, and he pushed her head into the curve of his shoulder and held her loosely, his hand stroking her hair, until she leaned quietly against him.

His lips touched her forehead, and she heard him murmur, 'Sweetheart, have you ever been with a man?'

She shook her head, feeling her face grow hot, glad that she didn't have to look at him.

His chest rose and fell in a sigh, and he moved her away from him. Catherine couldn't read the look in his eyes. Then he tipped her chin with his hand and dropped a kiss quickly on her mouth before he left her.

In her mind she had relived that kiss over and over again before their next meeting.

They had gone to a show, and when he stopped the car outside the door of the flat she shared with

two friends, and drew her into his arms, she went
stiff with nervous tension.

'Stop it,' he chided, and shook her gently. 'I
won't do anything you don't want, Catherine.
Come on, darling—kiss me.'

She lifted her face mutely, and he studied it with
a strange enigmatic expression. 'Please,' he said at
last, 'kiss me.'

He bent his head and she met his lips softly,
surprised to find them undemanding, gentle,
almost tentative, as though he was afraid of
frightening her. She relaxed, trusting him, yearning
strangely for a closer contact, and Jason pulled her
into his arms and her head rested against the seat
back as his mouth firmed and took hers with
passion.

Later, as she made a reluctant movement away
from him, he said, 'I love you. Marry me—please!'

It jolted her. She hadn't thought of marriage.
She had scarcely thought of loving him. She said
shakenly, 'I don't know . . . I never thought of you
being in love with me . . .'

'Isn't it obvious?' He sounded dry, and
Catherine shook her head.

She said, 'I've no idea what you're thinking,
most of the time. You're very—controlled.'

She heard the uneven breath of his laughter. 'I
try to be,' he said. 'It isn't easy when I'm around
you.'

She experienced a peculiar thrill at the admission. She knew she was nice to look at, attractive
to men. They had told her often enough, and there
was the evidence of her mirror. But she had never
heard quite that note in a man's voice before. Even
her body responded to it, with a soft uncurling of
desire.

It made examining her own emotions dispassionately very difficult. 'I don't know,' she said again. 'Give me time.'

He had given her time, but not a lot, and although he didn't force the issue, his lovemaking had been an insistent though patient wearing down of her defences. Once she had tentatively tried to indicate that she felt it clouded the issue, and Jason looked at her with his eyes narrowed slightly, his mouth wry, and said, 'I'm a man, Catherine, and I'm as circumspect as you've any right to expect. I promised I won't ravish you, you can trust me on that. I'm hanged if I'm going to accept a complete "hands off" policy from you. It's more than I can take.'

She supposed it was unfair to ask it of him, but at times she suspected that he knew very well what a potent weapon his lovemaking was, and that he used it deliberately, in spite of his considerable discretion, which she had to admit.

In the end he had won. She had married him, loved him, borne his children. He had fought his way to the top in his profession, a man driven by a desire to succeed that sometimes left her wondering if his wife and children were only a sort of fringe benefit. She had learned to be an executive wife and a social hostess, making small talk and canapés with equal skill and a degree of boredom, and glad to escape into motherhood when the children came, able to absorb herself in their needs to a great extent, dodging the social and business functions when she could, still playing the gracious hostess when she must, being the faithful, loyal helpmeet, but feeling that her life had some deeper purpose in the terribly important work of shaping two young lives towards happiness and fulfilment.

On their honeymoon, Jason's passion had almost frightened her, and he had learned to temper it with tenderness, to adjust to her different, more uncertain responses. But before long he had taught her a passion nearly equal to his own, and they had enjoyed a marvellous sexual rapport, scarcely interrupted by the birth of Michael. In fact, that had seemed to bring a new dimension into their lovemaking, as Jason had become more sensitive to her need for rest and care, and she had experienced a kind of loving gratitude to her husband for the new, wonderful son he had given her.

But Jenny's birth had been more difficult, and Catherine's recovery slower. It was a long time before she felt able to welcome Jason again, and when she did turn to him she had been unable to summon the response that he had become accustomed to arousing. Once she had resorted to pretence, and he had known and been furious. It was the only time she had ever thought he might be close to violence, and she had cringed and cried. Jason had stared disbelievingly at her for several seconds, and then pulled on his robe and left the room. He didn't return until morning, and she supposed he had slept in the spare room they kept for visitors.

For a time, she was too tired to care that he had ceased making love to her, until she realised with a jolt one day that it was months since he had touched her. She gave the children an early meal, cooked a special dinner for herself and Jason, and donned a new patio dress before he came home, spraying perfume on her body and behind her ears.

He had watched her, narrow-eyed, throughout the meal, making her nervous, and when he had helped her do the dishes, he waited as though he expected her to make the first move. And she made it, a little later, after leading the way into the lounge where he sat on the long expensive sofa and she sank down at his feet, leaning her head against his knees, and allowed her hand to slide along his thigh.

He took a long, shuddering breath and grasped her hand in his, and, bending his head, put his lips to her palm. Catherine looked up and saw that he had his eyes tightly shut, while his mouth pressed hotly on her skin, and she trembled.

He looked up, and his eyes held hers, a leaping fire in their depths. 'I hope you mean it,' he said thickly. 'I hope to God you mean it.'

She didn't answer, but twisted and got up on her knees to face him, her arms going round his neck. He pulled her up on to his lap and kissed her fiercely, then got up, swinging her high against his chest, and carried her to their bed.

He was not gentle, he almost threw her on to the mattress before he followed her down, and his hands on the lovely dress tore the stitching as he dispensed with it. His kisses bruised her skin, but sent a sudden hot tide of desire racing through her veins, and she arched herself to him as he tore off his own clothing, touching his hair and clutching at his head as it rested heavily against her breast.

He scooped a hand into her hair, and held her, his eyes blazing down at her face, his voice exultant. 'You want me! You do, don't you?'

'Yes,' she whispered, gasping and gulping with the force of her desire. 'Yes, Jason, oh yes!'

'Now?' His voice was deep and rasping with passion.

'Yes—now!'

When he came to her, violently and deeply, she cried out and writhed beneath him with sudden pleasure.

'Does it hurt?' he asked hoarsely, raising his head. 'Did I hurt you?'

Her head moved restlessly in negation, her parted lips saying words she barely heard herself. 'Yes,' she said, 'yes, hurt me!' She pulled him to her with her arms about his neck, with an overwhelming need to feel every physical sensation he could give her, to a pitch where pain and pleasure had no dividing line, and the hard fingers digging into the flesh of her shoulders were one with the passion of the mouth that closed over hers, the heavy body that crushed her breasts and the driving force that was the apex of this voluptuous, intoxicating torture.

Jason laughed softly against her ear, and bit it, and she shuddered in ecstasy. Then the vortex took her, swirled her into a giddy, incredible, mindless rush of sheer brilliant feeling, weightless, wonderful, too much to bear alone, so that she clung to Jason's shoulders, imploring him to hold her, to stay with her. And felt him, too, plunge into the whirlpool with her, until together they reached a quieter shore.

They were both panting, spent, and it was a long time before they could move apart, reluctantly loosing themselves from each other's arms.

Catherine, still faintly dizzy, lay with her arm over her eyes. She didn't know just what had happened to her. She had never felt like that before. The violence of the encounter shocked her in retrospect. She felt slightly ashamed of her own bold enjoyment, the demands she had made, the things she had said.

In the morning, she had avoided Jason's puzzled gaze. It had never been like that again. Not in all the years since. They made love, not as often as before—she assumed that was normal in any marriage after several years and two children—but frequently enough, and she responded less wildly than that night, perhaps less passionately than she had in the honeymoon period, but adequately, she supposed. Jason seemed satisfied, and she—she enjoyed his lovemaking. There were times when she felt an unease, almost a discontent, that bothered her, briefly. She would thrust it away, tell herself that she had everything to be grateful for, a nice home, a lovely family, no financial worries, a husband who was successful and considerate, a good father and a good lover. It was true that he worked long hours, that he was frequently late home and not infrequently away for days or weeks at a time, for his job entailed some travelling, and she had stopped going with him since the children . . .

Sometimes she wondered if he slept alone on those business trips. She knew that a secretary often accompanied him, that there were women among the people that he met, some of them glamorous, some of them, no doubt, available. There were times when he seemed preoccupied, and she worried that they were growing apart. Even when he brought her gifts from his trips, a bracelet or a bottle of perfume, occasionally flowers, she fought down a suspicion that his conscience was prompting him. He was a passionate man. She had seen other women sizing him up, assessing him. She knew they were attracted to him. And sometimes something deep inside her whispered that she had disappointed him . . .

He had never said so, never indicated that it was so. Catherine told herself that she was merely suffering from a residue of the diffidence that had plagued her early in their marriage, when she had felt herself to be too young and inadequate.

They had a good marriage, a perfectly normal, happy marriage. If some of the romance and excitement had gone out of it, that was only to be expected. One didn't live on a pinnacle of sensual pleasure and romantic happiness for ever.

And yet, at only twenty-six, Catherine found herself thinking, with a claustrophobic sense of panic, *Is this all? Is this my life? Jason's wife, Michael's and Jenny's mother?* Sometimes she had the feeling that she was not a person at all, but only an appendage to other people's lives. Jason's, Michael's and Jenny's. She had been Mrs Clyde for eight years, 'Mummy' to two children for the past six. What had happened to Catherine Vaughan, single person?

There were days when she wondered if Catherine Vaughan had ever existed.

CHAPTER TWO

THE plane was a small dark blot against the distant sky, and the wind blew coldly, making Catherine's eyes water. She turned and made her way downstairs and through the terminal building, among returning travellers and departing ones laden with luggage, and went through the automatic doors to the outside again. She found her car in the car-park after some hunting, because she had forgotten to note where she had parked it. Jason would have been able to go straight to it, if he had been with her. He never missed that kind of detail. It contributed to his success, she supposed, tiredly.

She felt let down, at a loose end. No children for seven weeks. The days stretched ahead of her yawningly, incredibly hard to fill.

That was stupid, of course. There was the pantomime, for a start. And Jason had suggested they take a few days' break, when he could spare the time. He was free over Christmas and New Year, but she had the pantomime then. Still, without the children to look after or find babysitters for, they could spend some time together . . .

She unlocked the car and got in. She liked driving, and Jason had bought the little car for her use. She ran the children about in it on weekdays for their dancing and swimming lessons and Michael's Cub Scout meetings, and did her shopping on Wednesday mornings. Jason had the big car which they used on the weekends for family outings. When Jason could spare the time.

She switched on the ignition, took a quick glance in the rear vision mirror and backed out of the parking space—and there was a horrible jolt and the dreadful sound of tearing, crushing metal.

She slammed on the brake, jerking forward against her safety belt. Sick with fright, she released the belt and looked behind her, twisting her head to peer out of the side window.

She had no idea where the other car had come from, but she had backed into it, crushing the mudguard of the right front wheel against the tyre. Gingerly she eased her car forward, wincing as she heard the protest of the metal.

She climbed out and saw the driver of the other car try to open his door, give up and slide out the other side.

Surveying the damage, Catherine saw that it was worse than she had thought. She had dented the driver's door as well as the mudguard. She would never have believed she could make that much of a mess just backing out at five miles an hour.

'I'm terribly sorry!' she apologised. 'I'm afraid it was my fault. I just didn't see you!'

An amused male voice said, 'That's obvious! I don't flatter myself you did it on purpose.'

She looked for the first time at his face, and saw that he was young and brown-haired, and certainly good-looking, and his blue eyes were resting with blatant male appreciation on her face.

'Flatter——?' she murmured, bewildered.

'To get to meet me,' he explained.

'Oh.' Stupidly, she felt herself blushing, and saw the amusement in the blue eyes deepen.

She had been standing with her hands clasped, fighting an absurd desire to wring them. His eyes flickered down, noting the gold band and the diamond solitaire on her left hand, and he gave her a comically rueful smile. 'Sorry,' he said. 'My sense of humour gets out of hand. Well, what are we going to do about this?'

'We—exchange names and addresses, don't we?' she suggested. 'I'm insured.'

'A pleasure,' he said, taking a notebook and gold propelling pencil from the breast pocket of his smart dark rust suit. He scribbled down his name and address and tore the page out to give it to her, and then wrote down hers.

'It's good of you to take it so well,' Catherine said gratefully, as he closed the book.

'I don't bawl out pretty girls,' he assured her cheerfully. 'Even if they happen to be married.' He turned and frowned at his damaged car. 'I don't think I'll be able to drive that far, though. The metal is scraping on the wheel.' He tried to shift the twisted piece, but it obstinately sprang back.

'Were you going in to Auckland?' she asked. 'Could I give you a lift?'

'I was.'

'Then please—it's the least I can do.'

'Well, do you have time to wait while I get something done about this?' He indicated his car. 'I can't just leave it there like that. It'll have to be picked up for repair.'

'Of course.'

'Sure?' he persisted.

'Yes. I've just seen my two children off on a flight to Sydney. I'm at a loose end for the rest of the day.'

The look he gave her was shrewd. 'Take your mind off missing them, eh?'

Catherine smiled. 'They'll only be away for seven weeks. But yes, it would.'

'You're on,' he grinned. 'Stay here, I'll be right back.'

Her car would need a modest amount of panelbeating, too, she realised, as he strode off. She got into the driver's seat and looked properly at the scrap of paper he had given her. Russel Thurston, it said. Russel with one L. It suited him.

He came back with a traffic controller who helped him to push his car out of the way. He picked up a small bag and swung it into the back seat of Catherine's car. 'You're sure this is okay?'

'Quite sure.' She was firm, smiling at him as he took the passenger seat beside her and folded his long legs into the space before him.

'Fasten your safety belt,' she reminded him crisply as she backed, much more cautiously this time. He obeyed, casting her a quizzical look and saying, 'Yes, ma'am.'

Catherine bit her lip and smiled apologetically. 'I usually drive my kids,' she explained. 'It's an automatic reflex.'

'How old are they?'

She told him, and he whistled. 'You must have been married from your cradle!'

'Nonsense. I was nineteen.'

He grimaced. 'Pretty young. I'm twenty-seven and *I'm* too young to be married.'

Catherine smiled. 'It's different for a man.'

'Is it? I don't see why.'

He seemed to expect an answer, and she said, 'Well, because—because women mature earlier.'

'So how old was your husband?'

She cast him a surprised look, and he held up a hand and said, 'Sorry, I don't mean to be personal.'

'He was thirty,' she said.

He shifted as though she had startled him, and

she glanced at him in time to see his lips purse as though he was about to whistle again. But he didn't. Instead, he gazed ahead of them at the wide road, and kept total silence.

Driven to it, against her will and better judgment, Catherine said defensively, 'It's not such a huge difference. We're very happy.'

She felt his sharp stare as though it was a rapier. The hum of the motor seemed very loud. Then he said quietly, 'Congratulations.'

What was she doing, explaining her marriage to a total stranger? This was a crazy conversation to be having. 'Are you a psychiatrist?' she asked him.

He laughed. 'No. I'm in television. A producer, though I have done some reporting in my murky past.'

'Should I have recognised you?'

'No. I haven't appeared before the cameras much. My work is behind the scenes. My name comes up on the credits, but most people hardly notice that.'

'Don't you like the cameras?' She looked at him curiously. He would look good on film, and he had a pleasant voice too, cultured, not affected, and with an attractive masculine timbre.

'I prefer making things happen,' he said. 'I got tired of reporting. The production side is more interesting.'

'What programmes have you worked on?'

He told her, and she recognised the names of some programmes which she had liked. When she told him so, he seemed pleased.

'What about you?' he asked her. 'Are you a full-time mum? Or do you have a job, too?'

'No—yes. I mean, yes, no.' She laughed. 'I can't claim mothering takes all my time, now. But I don't have a job. I thought about it, but . . .'

'Your husband doesn't approve?'

'It isn't that exactly. But we don't need the money, and I'm not trained for anything.'

'So what do you do with your time?'

'Various things.' She told him about the art class, making a funny story of her failure, and he laughed delightedly. Then she described the pantomime, and he watched her face as she talked, asked her questions about the production, the costumes, the dialogue. She sang one of the ditties that she had written for it, a wicked little spoof on a well-known song, with some comic references to current events. His enjoyment of it was obvious, and he asked, 'Do you do much of that sort of thing?'

'This is the first time. It was fun, though.'

'I'd like to see the show.'

'You don't mean that. An amateur panto?'

'I don't say things I don't mean. It sounds great. Is it only for the hospital patients?'

'And a few members of their familes. If you're really interested——'

'Yes?' he prompted, as she hesitated. 'Could you sneak me in if I disguised myself in bandages, do you think?'

She smiled. 'No. I was wondering, if you had the time, if you'd like to come along some time and give us some advice. As a professional.'

'I'd love to. If your producer won't mind.'

'I can guarantee she'll be delighted. We're all beginners at this, apart from one or two of the singers who have some experience.'

'Tell me when. I'll try to be there.'

'That's a rash promise. Aren't you busy?'

'I have to drop a take in at the studio, then I'm officially on holiday for the next three weeks. Can I give you lunch?'

Catherine looked surprised, and a little wary.

'No strings,' he said. 'Husband wouldn't approve?'

She didn't know if Jason would 'approve'. This situation had never arisen before.

'Lunch,' Russel Thurston said. 'In a public place. You said you were at a loose end.'

'I'd like to have lunch with you,' she said. 'If I'm allowed to pay my share.' She felt slightly reckless, but where was the harm in it? She liked him. He liked her, but he wasn't coming on with any sexual invitations, by word or look. Of course he had noticed she was female, had said frankly that he thought her a pretty woman, but there it had stopped. No suggestive glances, no 'accidental' touches. He was a nice man. Safe.

He was smiling at her again. He had a very attractive smile.

'Are you a liberated lady?' he teased her.

She made a little grimace. 'Hardly. I'm the typical suburban housewife, with my regulation two point five children, a cabbage of the worst kind.'

'You're no cabbage,' he said, amused. Then, his eyes sweeping over her slimness, he repeated, 'Two point five?'

'I didn't mean that,' she said hastily. 'It was a figure of speech.'

He grinned. 'A pigeon pair, are they? A boy and a girl?' She nodded, and he said, 'Sounds like you've got it made, lady.'

'Yes, doesn't it?' Catherine heard the bitter note in her voice, was immediately shocked at herself. Why had she sounded like that? Russel Thurston had noticed, too. He had that look again, *I'm not saying a word, but* . . .

Involuntarily, she said, 'Don't do that!'

He looked startled. 'What?'

'Don't look at me like that. I am perfectly . . .'.

As her voice tailed off, he looked at her unsmilingly. 'Tell me again how happy you are,' he said softly. 'I'm not arguing.'

Catherine bit her lip. This was ridiculous. It wasn't happening. How could a man she had met less than half an hour ago be dredging up feelings she had scarcely known about, herself? Simply by saying nothing?

She kept her eyes on the road. There was more traffic now. They had crossed the long bridge at Mangere, over the arm of the Manukau, skirted Onehunga, and climbed the slope to pass One Tree Hill with its obelisk and crowning tree.

She drew up at a red traffic light and said, 'Maybe lunch isn't such a good idea.'

He waited until the lights were green and the car was moving forward. 'What's changed in the last ten minutes?' he asked quietly.

'My mind.'

He laughed. His look at her was speculative. 'I'm no danger to you, Catherine,' he said. 'I don't go round preying on frustrated married ladies——'

'I am *not* frustrated!' she snapped. She had noticed his use of her name, found it strangely intimate, disturbing.

'Fine,' he said, and his voice had hardened slightly. 'Then stop being so silly, and have lunch with me.'

He had knocked her off balance with that. She slowed for another set of lights, picked up speed as they flicked from red to green, and asked, almost humbly, '*Am* I being silly?'

Gently, he said, 'Yes, you are, rather. You said you'd like it—lunch together. So why deprive yourself? Change your mind again.'

'All right,' she said after a moment. 'Where to? We're nearly in city centre.'

He directed her to the studio car-park, into the space reserved for his own car. 'Come in?' he invited. 'Have a look around?'

She was tempted, but shook her head, shyness intervening. There would be people there, his workmates, wondering who she was, what she was doing with him. Really, it was simple enough to explain. She had pranged his car, given him a lift. Anyone would have done the same. Still, she stayed in her seat. 'I'll wait,' she said.

'Promise?'

She withdrew a little, invisibly. It wasn't that important.

She saw his eyes on the keys in the ignition, but he removed his gaze to look at her. 'Be here when I get back,' he said. He turned to collect his bag, and got out.

He wasn't away long. When he returned, he didn't get into the car but said, 'I know a place not too far away. Would you like to leave the car here and walk? It saves finding parking.'

Catherine agreed, and slid out of her seat with his hand lightly on her arm. He withdrew it as soon as she had straightened, and only touched her again as they crossed the road, when his fingers curved about her elbow for a few moments.

The restaurant was small and clean, brightly decorated for the luncheon trade. They had crisp salads and crusty French bread with cold meats, then strong, pungently dark coffee afterwards. And they talked. Catherine talked. She didn't remember when anyone had taken such a blatant interest in what she had to say. She felt herself sparkling all over, suddenly more alive than she seemed to have been in months—years.

They had lingered over the coffee, and when she glimpsed his watch and checked her own, alarmed, her first thought was that she must get home before the children.

Of course, the children were not coming home, she could stay indefinitely if she wanted, but the sparkle evaporated. She became anxious and jittery, and said she had to go.

Russ—most people called him that, he said—didn't argue. He let her pay her share of the bill, his grin a little rueful, and then he went with her back to her car.

'Can I drop you somewhere?' she asked him, half fearful that he would accept, although another part of her wanted to prolong the delightful companionship they had shared.

His look was assessing, thoughtful. She fancied he could read her indecision. 'No, thanks, Cathy,' he said. 'Don't forget to let me know when I can come to a rehearsal of the pantomime, will you?'

She smiled, relieved, not analysing the relief. 'I'll call you,' she said. Cathy. Nobody had called her Cathy since her schooldays. Russ said it easily, as if he had known her even then.

Crazy, she told herself as she drove through the busy streets, going home. Crazy. Having lunch with a man she had never met before. Telling him—what had she told him? Silly things about her childhood, about her early, nervous attempts at entertaining as a young bride, stories about Michael and Jenny. She must have bored him. Who wanted to hear stories about the cute sayings of other people's children? But he hadn't been bored. He had laughed, questioned, commented, encouraged. And told stories in his turn, about his work, the personalities he met, the people he had

interviewed in his reporting days. It had been—
nice. Really a nice afternoon. Her mouth kept
curving into a smile as she remembered his
anecdote, that remark. When she got home she
would phone Bridie Hawkins, who, with help
from all and sundry, was the nominal producer
of the show, ask her when Russ could look in on
them.

'You look better already,' said Jason, after he had
kissed her. He had come in while she was mixing a
salad for their evening meal, his briefcase still in
his hand. He stepped back and surveyed her,
making the unexpected comment.

'Better?' Catherine repeated.

'You've been looking tired lately.'

Had she? 'I don't know why,' she said. 'With
the children both at school, I'm not exactly
overworked. There's far less to do than when they
were babies.'

'You've been spending a lot of time at the
hospital, though, haven't you? Did they get off all
right? No floods of tears?'

'Not really,' she said sadly, and as he looked at
her sharply, 'No. Michael shed one small one.
Jenny was very brave.'

Jason smiled. 'You too?'

'Me too. Only I——'

He had his hand under her chin, preparing to
kiss her again. 'Yes?' he said.

'Nothing. I'll tell you later.'

His brows went up a little, and he let his hand
drop and turned away.

Over their coffee, Catherine told him, 'I had
lunch with Russel Thurston.'

'Who?'

'Russel Thurston. He's a television producer.'

'Oh, yes. He did *Flames of Fury*.'

'How did you know that?'

Jason looked amused. 'His name was on every episode. He's good. I didn't know you knew him.'

'I ran into his car at the airport.'

'What?' His brows drew together.

'It's all right. The damage wasn't very bad, and the insurance will take care of it, won't it?'

'That's not the point!'

'I know, I'm sorry. I suppose I wasn't concentrating, but I *did* look in the rear-view mirror, and honestly I could have sworn the way was clear.'

'Stop making excuses, Catherine!'

She looked down at her half-empty coffee cup and was silent. He sounded exasperated.

Jason said violently, 'I'm not bothered about the damage to the cars—yours or his. Or what caused it. Are *you* all right?'

'Yes, of course.' Her voice was husky with surprise and residual hurt. He had been concerned about *her*. She felt guilty, abased. 'You said yourself I was looking—well.'

'Yes.' He relaxed, the frown easing.

'I'm sorry, Jason.'

He shook his head impatiently. 'It doesn't matter. As long as you're all right.'

'No one was hurt. It was a silly accident. But he couldn't drive his car after it, so I gave him a lift into Auckland.'

'And had lunch.'

'Yes. I paid for mine.'

'Did you? How liberated of you!'

She looked up at him, smiling. 'That's what Russ said——'

Jason was watching her rather intently.

She stared again at her coffee cup, picked up the

spoon in the saucer and put it down. Jason said, 'What are you trying to tell me, Catherine?'

'Nothing.' She looked up again, disconcerted by the keen gaze he was bending on her. 'Just about meeting someone interesting, having lunch with him, that's all. It was—pleasant.'

'Pleasant?'

'Yes.' She met his eyes with defiance in the sparkling green of hers. 'Are you jealous?'

'Should I be?'

'No.'

'Then I'm not jealous. You gave a man a lift, had lunch with him, enjoyed it. Fine. I'm glad you enjoyed it. Have lunch with *me*, one day.'

'Could we? That would be nice.'

'Yes, I think it would.' He smiled, then said, 'But not this week. I'm tied up every day.'

The warm glow of surprised pleasure she had felt faded a little. 'Next week, then,' she said brightly, wondering if he would remember, or if he would get 'tied up' again.

Suddenly she was tired. Lunch had been an interlude, a few hours of fantasy, of being a person in her own right, not somebody's wife, somebody else's mother, but a person that another person could take an interest in for her own sake. A woman that a man wanted to take to lunch, wanted to talk to, wanted to listen to, liked looking at.

She had lunched with Jason before, when he was entertaining clients or business colleagues. And sometimes she had met him with the children for lunch. She couldn't remember the last time they had met for lunch alone, away from home. Before Michael was born, probably.

Tomorrow—what was she doing tomorrow? The refrigerator needed cleaning. She ought to do that. She had been letting stocks get low in the freezer compartment so that there wouldn't be much to leave out while the job was done. She could go out and buy some more frozen foods to restock it. Not that they would need a lot while the children were away.

Tomorrow was another day. Another day like so many other days that had gone before it.

Except this day. This day, today, had been different.

Catherine went to bed early, missing the nightly battle of sending the children off for a bath, checking that after all the flooding of the bathroom floor, and disintegration of the soap in murky water, the wringing wet towels and the reluctance to get out following an even greater reluctance to get in, they had actually managed to get some of the soap and water on themselves. And she missed reading the story that Jenny still insisted on, and that Michael pretended not to be listening to.

She settled into bed and turned the reading lamp on, opening a thriller she had borrowed from the library, but the plot didn't hold her. She thought about Jenny and Michael turning to wave to her before they disappeared with the smiling stewardess who had shepherded them away from her. And about Russel Thurston saying, 'Tell me again how happy you are.'

Jason came in. He looked over at her and said, 'In bed already? Tired?'

'A bit.'

He seemed to hesitate before he walked over to the bed and sat on it, turning her book so that he could see the cover.

'Bloodthirsty tastes you have,' he commented, raising his brows at the gory picture of a half-nude blonde girl with a dagger in her heart.

'It's not as bad as that, really. You can't judge a book by its cover.'

'Now, there's an original remark!'

'You like it? It's yours.'

'Gee, thanks,' he said dryly, making her smile.

He smiled, too, then reached his hand around behind her and pulled her close to kiss her. His mouth touched her gently, a question in his kiss.

Catherine found her mind diving here and there, behind her closed eyes images of the plane disappearing into the distance, Michael wiping a surreptitious tear on his sleeve, Russ with his fingers just touching her elbow as they crossed the road . . . and Jason frowning, saying, 'It doesn't matter, as long as you're all right.'

The mouth on hers became firmer, wanting an answer, and a warm trickle of response began to flow from her thighs upward through her body. Her lips were acceptant, quiescent, but just as she was about to obey the sluggishly awakened impulse to return his kiss, Jason lifted his mouth from hers and said, 'You'd better not read too long. Get some sleep. I've got work to do in the study.'

At the door he said goodnight to her, and she automatically returned it. She read hardly a chapter before she put out the light to court the sleep that wouldn't come. But a long time before Jason came to join her, oblivion overtook her at last.

CHAPTER THREE

BRIDIE had been delighted at the idea of having a real live TV producer along to give his advice on the production of the pantomime. 'Fantastic!' she had said. 'How did you manage to get hold of him?'

'Accidentally,' Catherine admitted. 'I backed into his car.'

Bridie shrieked, laughing. 'You didn't! Wow, that's what I call enterprising!'

'I told you, it was an accident,' Catherine protested, smiling. Bridie was irrepressible, bubbling over with *joie de vivre*, always ready for a laugh. She had five children, four of them teenagers, the youngest a little older than Michael, and she managed to handle her family with apparent ease while still finding time to play tennis once a week, and serve on a school committee, help take meals on wheels to old folk, and be secretary of the swimming club, as well as take part in the hospital visiting and producing the pantomime. She was plump and freckled with a halo of frizzed sandy hair framing a perpetual friendly, rather mischievous smile, and Catherine admired her greatly, envying her energy and her capacity for enjoyment. The admiration was shared by Bridie's husband. Paul Hawkins was a dark, quiet, thin man who was a company secretary—one of the best, according to Jason. Beside his effervescent wife he seemed ready to fade into the wallpaper, but those who got to know him discovered a puckish sense of humour

38

and a sincere interest in other people that made him a very good friend.

Bridie said, 'Does Jason know you go about bumping into strange men?'

'I don't make a habit of it. Do you want to meet him or not?'

'Of course I do! When can he come?'

'Tell me when it suits you, and I'll phone him. Better still, I'll give you his number and you can arrange it yourself.'

'No, no. You know the rehearsal nights. Any time will do me just fine.'

So Catherine made the arrangement, and was warmed by the pleasure in Russel Thurston's voice when she told him who was speaking. It was only a short conversation, but he said he was looking forward to seeing her again, and she reciprocated before putting down the receiver.

He strolled into the rehearsal looking handsome and casual in dress jeans and an open-necked blue knitted cotton shirt. They were doing a scene in which Catherine, as the Good Fairy, figured quite prominently. She faltered when he came in, and the rest of the cast stared, but he shook his head and said, 'Please carry on, sorry to interrupt.'

He leaned against the wall until they had finished. Then Catherine introduced him to Bridie and the others, and Bridie asked eagerly, 'What do you think?'

Russel grinned at her. 'I've only watched one scene. Could I see a copy of the script, do you think?'

'Yes, of course.' She handed him her own copy, and they were soon huddled over it together, making notes on the pages and firing quick questions and answers at each other. Watching them, Catherine noticed his lightning comprehension, his absorption in Bridie's queries, his close attention to her comments. He was giving her as much respect as if she was a professional like himself. She had been half fearful that he would patronise them all as amateurs, and also there had been a sneaking, uneasy feeling in the back of her mind that really he had made this an excuse to see her again.

Wryly, she admitted to herself that he scarcely seemed to have noticed her at all. Obviously he was serious in his desire to help.

After twenty minutes they ran through the scene again, and this time Russel stood beside Bridie, and every now and then they would hold up the action and confer together.

At one point Russel came on to the improvised stage, and began to alter the positions of the cast. He gently ushered two little girls playing junior fairies a few paces to the left, with his hands on their shoulders, and then took Catherine's arm and moved her forward a little, positioning her exactly where he thought she should stand, with two firm hands briefly on her waist. 'There!' he said to Bridie, still standing by Catherine, so that she felt his breath stir her hair. 'How's that?'

'Much better!' Bridie approved. 'Can you all remember those positions?'

'We can mark them until they do,' Russel suggested. 'Got some chalk?'

A few sticks were produced, and he made the marks himself after commanding them to keep still. Catherine glanced down at the slightly ruffled brown hair as he made a white cross at her feet, and as he straightened he caught her eye and smiled at her. He was quite close when he stood up, and the moment took on a peculiar intimacy.

Later, after the rest of the cast had left, he and

Bridie were still discussing some points for improvement, while Catherine hovered nearby. Bridie turned to her and said, 'Oh, Catherine, I'm sorry! I didn't mean to hold you up.' Turning to Russel, she explained, 'I brought Catherine along in my car, we usually come together. I could talk to you all night, but——'

Russel smiled. 'What about us all having some coffee some place? I haven't nearly finished talking to you, either.'

'Well, it's late,' Bridie said doubtfully. 'Tell you what, why don't you come and have coffee at my place? You, too, Catherine. You've brought a car?' she asked Russel.

'Yes. I'll follow you. Unless Catherine could come with me and show me the way, perhaps?'

He smiled at Catherine, and Bridie said, 'Good idea. If Jason will be worried, you can phone him from my place, Catherine. Come on then, we'll lock up here and be on our way.'

In Russel's car, Catherine snapped on her safety belt and said, 'It looks as good as new, doesn't it? I'm glad the damage has been repaired so promptly.'

'It's fine. There were no problems.'

'The insurance company said it was quite straightforward. They weren't too pleased, though.'

He grinned. 'Too bad. That's what they're for.'

'Thank you for coming. It's meant a lot to Bridie—and all of us.'

'Don't thank me. I wanted to do it. She's quite a lady, isn't she?'

'She certainly is.' She told him about some of Bridie's other activities, and he whistled, impressed. 'No suburban neurosis there,' he commented.

'No. Bridie wouldn't have time for that sort of luxury.'

'What about you?' he asked, adding, as she turned her head to him, 'Not that I'm suggesting you're neurotic! But are you finding time on your hands, while your children are away?'

'I've cleaned the house from top to bottom and side to side,' she admitted. 'And there isn't a weed left in the garden. I've even mended all the children's clothes.'

'And darned your husband's socks?'

She laughed. 'He wears nylon, thank goodness. Turn left here.'

He swung the wheel, and was silent for a few minutes. Catherine asked, 'Are you enjoying your holiday? Have you been away?'

'I hope to get away next week. This week I've been tying up loose ends, cleaning out my study at home.' He gave a mock groan. 'The stuff I've accumulated, you've no idea!'

'Are you a hoarder?'

'I must be. I found an old school tie among the junk—and it wasn't even my school!'

As she laughed, he asked her, 'Do you hoard, too? Do we turn left or right here?'

'Sorry. Right,' she said. 'I used to keep everything on the principle that it might come in useful someday, but Jason's nearly cured me. He hates clutter, and he's quite ruthless.'

'So does my mother. I think she was delighted when I fled the nest—or is it flew? Anyway, she was glad to see me go.'

'I bet she wasn't!'

'How do you know I'm not impossible to live with?'

'You?' she said gaily. 'Never! You're far too nice.'

There was an odd little silence, and then Russel said quite soberly, 'Well, thank you.'

'Right again at the next corner,' she said hastily. She had embarrassed him, and herself. And that was silly. Why shouldn't a woman pay a man a perfectly sincere compliment now and then? She said, 'Please don't be embarrassed.'

'I'm not. I'm—delighted. You're a pretty nice person yourself, Mrs Clyde.'

'It's number twenty-seven,' she told him. 'Just here.'

They had lost Bridie's car some way back, but the porch light was on and she could see that the Austin was already drawn up in the carport. Russel stopped his car in front of the gate, and switched off the headlights. Catherine wondered if he had called her Mrs Clyde to put some distance between them. Had he thought she was trying to flirt with him?

She opened the door abruptly and scrambled out of the car. By the time he had locked his and come round to join her she had already pushed the gate wide and was halfway to the front door of the house.

Bridie opened the door before they reached it, welcoming them in. She had the coffee already percolating, she said, and Paul wanted to meet Russel.

The two men talked while Bridie returned to the kitchen and Catherine phoned Jason. 'I'll be later than usual,' she told him. 'I'm staying for coffee at Bridie's.'

'Okay,' he said easily. 'Have you got your key? I'm going to bed, I'm whacked.'

He sounded tired. 'I've got a key,' she said. 'Don't worry about me.'

She hadn't told him Russel was here, too. As she went back to the kitchen and helped Bridie butter biscuits and fill the four cups, she pushed

away a vague, stupid feeling of guilt. She was
having coffee at Bridie's. Jason neither needed nor
wanted a complete list of who else was here.

In the event, she talked mostly with Paul, while
the other two took out the script again and
continued their discussion on it. Now and then
Bridie called for her opinion, and once Russel
smiled across at her and asked her to take a look
at one of the alterations they had proposed for
her. It was nearly midnight when he closed the
folder holding the script, and pushed it away with
his empty cup, saying, 'I've kept you people up
long enough. I'd better be going.'

'It was awfully good of you to take the trouble,'
Bridie told him. 'I'll take you home now,
Catherine.'

'You needn't turn out again,' said Russel. 'I'd
be glad to drop Catherine off.'

'Oh, well——' Bridie looked grateful. 'You
don't mind, Catherine?'

'Of course not. If it's on Russel's way?' She
turned to him.

He didn't answer directly, but put a hand lightly
on her waist and ushered her to the door, as they
said goodnight all round.

In the car, she said, remembering his address,
'It isn't on your way, is it? You shouldn't
bother——'

'It's no trouble. Once I'm in the car, what
difference does it make, five minutes here or there?
It saved Bridie taking hers out again.'

'Yes, I suppose so. Thank you.'

'It's no hardship. Don't thank me, Cathy.'

She turned her head quickly, and he glanced at
the movement and said, 'Do you object?'

'To what?'

'My calling you Cathy.'

She shook her head. 'No. You called me Mrs Clyde before. I thought——'

She stopped there, and he prompted her, his eyes frankly curious. 'What did you think?'

Catherine shook her head again, silently, and he repeated, 'What did you think? Tell me.'

He had slowed the car a little, and his voice was persuasive.

In a low voice, she said, 'That you did it as a reminder—to me.'

They were still travelling quite slowly, although his eyes were fixed on the road. For a few minutes he said nothing, then he spoke with deliberation. 'Perhaps I did it as a reminder to myself.'

She stopped herself from asking why he needed a reminder. It was a provocative question, and she wasn't ready for a shift in their relationship. She said, 'Shall I direct you?'

'No, I know my way,' he assured her. 'I have your address, remember.'

She had his, too, but she didn't bring up that fact. 'You said you were going away next week,' she reminded him. 'Where to?'

'Not very far,' he answered, accepting the change of subject without comment. 'I bought a piece of land up the west coast a while ago, and I'm building on it. I've actually got a reasonably habitable sort of place there, now, although I'm still working on the inside. I hope to spend the next couple of weeks putting in some of the linings and building a deck out from the living area.'

'A working holiday?'

'Yes, you bet. It's great out there, though, not far from town but wild and wonderful, I can walk along the beach for miles and not see a soul on a weekday. And when I get hot and sticky on the job, I strip off and have a swim in the surf.'

'It sounds good.'

'You like the sea?'

'Love it. I love the surf, and a wide beach with huge breakers beating in from the Tasman. Where is your bach?'

'Near Karekare. You know it?'

'Oh, yes. Fantastic.' Her voice was filled with envy.

'I'll tell you how to find it,' said Russel. 'If you have a spare day, come out and see me.'

The idea was instantly appealing. Catherine turned to smile at him, her breath drawn in delight. But then she hesitated. 'Oh, I don't think I should disturb your holiday,' she said. 'You don't mean it.'

'Of course I mean it. It isn't everyone I invite out there, you know. I'd like you to come, honestly.'

'Then—thank you. I won't promise, but—if there's a chance, I'd like to.'

Russel grinned at her. 'Good!' He accelerated a little, and began whistling one of the tunes from the pantomime. After a few minutes she began softly singing the words, and they finished, laughing, as he drew up outside the darkened house. He pulled on the handbrake but left the engine running.

'Your husband doesn't wait up?' he asked her.

'Not tonight, he said he was tired. Thanks for the lift.'

'Wait a minute. I'll draw you a diagram, so you can find me at the beach. There's no phone, but I'll be at the bach, or swimming.'

He drew a map for her on a page of his notebook, and handed it over. 'Come,' he said. 'I really want you to see it.'

Catherine thanked him without promising

anything, and went into the house, the folded paper held in her hand.

She thought that Jason had forgotten about taking her to lunch, but the week before Christmas, he said, 'What about our date? Is today all right?'

'Date?' She was barely awake, and he was sitting on the side of the bed, half turned to her, while he buttoned his shirt. They had made love the night before, and his mouth was softer, his eyes warmer than usual. He looked at her sleep-flushed face, let his eyes wander down to the low neck of her nightgown, and leaned over to drop an intimate kiss between her breasts. 'Lunch,' he reminded her. 'Will you meet me?'

'Oh. Yes, I thought you'd forgotten.'

'I hadn't forgotten. I just hadn't had a chance. Will you come to the office? About twelve?'

He kissed her mouth briefly and stood up, smiling down at her. Catherine smiled back, and stretched a little, making to get up.

'Stay there,' he told her. 'You don't get much chance for a lie-in when the children are home.'

'But I feel so lazy!'

'Enjoy it. Anyway, I like that picture of you to think about during the day. You look very sexy, with your hair spreading over the pillow, and the sheet down to your hips, and that silk thing scarcely covering your beautiful body.'

'Jason!' It wasn't really a protest, but even after eight years of marriage, he could still make her blush when he talked like that.

He laughed, and turned to the door, doing up his belt.

'Jason?' she said, rather wistfully.

'Yes?' His face had changed already. She could see that he was getting ready for the office. He seemed to assume an office face with his clothes, an unemotional, clever, rather stern face.

'*Do* you think about me during the day?'

His expression hardly altered. 'I find it very hard not to,' he answered, and then went on out to the kitchen.

Catherine heard him go, and stretched again, almost tempted to go back to sleep. She had to exert willpower to make herself get up and shower, then she contemplated her wardrobe, a warm happiness inside her at the thought of lunch in town with her husband. She wanted to look nice— not overdressed, but cool and elegant, a wife he could be proud of taking out.

By eleven o'clock she had washed and dried her hair, pinning it up in a sophisticated knot, combing out a few careful tendrils to soften the style. She was wearing high-heeled sandals and a softly flared dress with a wide round neck and fitting bodice, made of thin synthetic, green with a subtle pattern of leaves in shades of brown, and a scattering of tiny white daisy flowers. She had spent half an hour making up, using cosmetics that added a fine bloom to her skin and a pink sheen to her lips without giving them an obviously made-up look. A smudging of green eyeshadow made her eyes look larger and darker. Her eyebrows were naturally darker than her hair, not needing any enhancement, but she had carefully painted mascara on to the tips of her long lashes. She looked good, and felt good, and was just picking up a small white handbag, looking about for her car keys, when the telephone rang.

Even as she lifted the receiver and recited the number, she had a feeling of foreboding. Jason's voice, crisp, businesslike, said, 'Catherine? Thank heaven you haven't left yet. Look, darling, I'm terribly sorry, but something's come up. I can't make lunch after all.'

She went cold, suddenly, clutching at the receiver, her teeth gritted together.

'Catherine?' His voice sharpened. 'Can you hear me?'

'Yes,' she managed.

There was a silence. He was waiting for her to say something, that she didn't mind, that they could lunch another time. She didn't. She couldn't.

'I'm sorry,' he said again. 'I'll make it up to you, I promise. This is too bad, but it can't be helped.' Again there was a pause. Then, puzzled, he said, 'Catherine? Are you there?'

'Yes.'

'Are you all right? I know it's disappointing for you——'

'Don't keep apologising.' Her voice was cold, controlled. 'It was only a lunch, after all. Nothing important.'

'Good girl. I'll explain when I get home. I know you'll understand. Can we make tomorrow instead, perhaps?' Lowering his voice, he added, 'Or tonight—I'll take you out to dinner. Dining and dancing, you'll like that. We can make a night of it. So wear something special. Okay?'

Catherine swallowed on a hard lump, and said, 'Okay.'

'Fine. See you later, darling. Goodbye.' His voice was hurried.

He didn't wait for her answering goodbye, which was just as well, because she could scarcely speak. She fumbled the receiver back on its cradle, almost dropping it, her hand shaking. Shaking. Only now she recognised the emotion that had sent her suddenly rigid and ice-cold, and now had her trembling in its grip. Rage, pure, knife-sharp rage. She tried to quell it, clenching her fists at her sides, walking into the bedroom with calm, slow steps, towards the dressing table, its long mirror reflecting her full-length.

It didn't show, she realised dispassionately. No one would have known she was in a white temper such as she had never experienced in her life. She stopped, staring at herself. Portrait of a beautiful woman. She was, she realised, with a slight sense of surprise, quite beautiful. She had dressed and made up very carefully today, and perhaps anger added an extra sparkle to her eyes and a glow to her skin.

All dressed up and nowhere to go, she told herself cynically. Because 'something had come up,' and Jason had casually cancelled their arrangement, confident that she would not object, that she would be just as pleased to meet him tomorrow or any other day.

She went to the dressing table, looked broodingly down at the purse that still lay there, then swept it into a drawer, dusted a film of powder from the polished surface, and absently opened the lid of the little box in which she kept safety pins, nail scissors, and other odds and ends. There was a folded scrap of paper there, too. Catherine stared at it for a moment before she remembered what it was. The directions that Russel had given her to find his beach place. He would be there now. He had asked her to come.

She picked it up, fingered it, opened out the single fold. Then she slid the bag out of the drawer again, put the piece of paper in it, and opened another drawer, stopping to pull out a bright red satin bikini. Her movements swift and sure now, she crossed to the big wardrobe, slid open the doors and hooked down a canvas beach bag hanging at one side, dropped the bikini into it and then fetched a large soft towel from the linen closet in the hall, stuffing that into the bag, too. Five minutes later she was in the car, heading north and west through the city.

She concentrated fiercely on her driving at first, being extra cautious as she negotiated the traffic lights and found her way out into the western suburbs and then finally to rolling countryside, where dairy cows and fat white sheep grazed contentedly on the hillsides. When the road wound up into the Waitakere range with its houses hidden in little pockets carved from the dense native bush, and soared along the tops of the hills with their panoramic views of the city, she found her mind returning persistently to Jason's telephone call, replaying his words like a record going over and over the same groove.

'Something's come up ... Can we make it tomorrow instead? ... I'm sorry ... I'll make it up to you, I promise ... It can't be helped ... I know it's disappointing for you ... I know you'll understand ... I'll take you out to dinner ... Dining and dancing—you'll like that.

'Something's come up ...' He hadn't even told her what the something was. Some business hitch, obviously. Was it serious, that he had stood her up for it? Or did he just think that breaking a date with his wife didn't matter, even if the 'something' was some trivial little problem that could have waited until tomorrow?

Unfair. Jason wouldn't have done that to her for nothing. Whatever it was, he must have thought it was important. More important than her?

'Can we make it tomorrow, instead ...' Why ever not? He knew her days were empty, one was as

good as another. Even if she had had a committee meeting or a hospital visiting day, they wouldn't clash with his lunch time.

'I know it's disappointing for you ...' He'd sounded sorry for her, wasn't that something? What about him? Was he disappointed, too? Or merely sorry that she had missed out on a treat he had planned for her? He'd kept saying he was sorry ...

'I know you'll understand ...' Well, he was wrong there. She hadn't felt at all understanding, she had felt enraged and humiliated.

'I'll take you out to dinner tonight ...' As though she was Jenny, needing an extra treat to make up for one she had missed out on. As though she was a child ...

She hadn't reacted like a child, not visibly. She had been cool and adult and 'understanding' and told him it didn't matter.

And put down the receiver shaking with rage. Because it did matter. Somehow it mattered dreadfully. Why should he think that he could just casually make a date with her and equally casually break it? Why should he be so sure she would take it without making a fuss, accept his apology, agree to make it another time, feel grateful that he was offering her dinner and dancing to compensate?

'Because you're his *wife*, that's why!' she muttered to herself, her teeth clenched. Because wives were assumed to be able to take it, to be used to being pushed aside for more urgent matters, to being relegated to the less important side of their husbands' lives, to being taken for granted.

That's the way things are, Catherine reflected bitterly. You're married, you're supposed to understand when your husband has to break his promise to you, when he doesn't have time for you, when he's tired and irritable and unreasonable.

Unreasonable ... But wasn't she the one being unreasonable? Making a drama out of a simple little cancelled lunch. It wasn't even an anniversary, or anything special. They could just as easily do the very same thing on any other day. Why was she so upset, so angry?

'I don't *know*!' she murmured, her hands gripping the wheel as the car began the descent to the coast road. But there was no denying that she was—that the broken promise was a trigger for a whole lot of buried resentments coming to the surface in a gigantic, cataclysmic wave of anger.

CHAPTER FOUR

SHE had to park the car and walk the last two hundred yards to the bach, along a narrow, high path bordered by stiff marram grass and dark flax rearing six feet high. The small house stood on a slope overlooking the sea, the wide, flat, dun-coloured beach and the lazy rollers swinging into the long sweep of shoreline. A few tough, twisted trees snuggled about it, and as she drew near she could hear the sound of whistling and hammering.

She stopped for a minute to admire the view, the sunlight making diamonds in the water, and the white clouds spreading feathery strands across acres of blue. She couldn't walk fast because she had forgotten to change from her high-heeled sandals, donned for lunch in town with little walking, and the path was littered with small, flinty stones poking out of the sand.

She hitched the canvas bag on to her shoulder and turned to look again at the bach. It was small, sturdy-looking and new, a board and corrugated iron construction, simply shaped, the roof sloping from the sea view towards the hillside behind. She walked further up the path, on to a little porch, and peered into the open doorway. As she did so, the hammering and whistling stopped abruptly and a violent swear-word sliced the warm air.

Catherine laughed, her eyes searching the dim interior. Vaguely she could discern a room with a camp bed in one corner, a saw-horse in the middle of the floor and a pile of lining board stacked beside it. Across from her was a step-ladder, with

Russel sitting on the top step, holding a hammer in one hand and looking disgustedly at a jagged crack in the piece of board he had just fastened.

His head turned at her laughter, and with her eyes becoming accustomed to the change from the sun's brightness, Catherine caught his blank look of surprise when he saw her.

Suddenly diffident, she stood silently in the doorway, wondering if he had regretted his invitation, if he had not really meant her to come. The blank look disconcerted her. Then he jumped lightly down from the ladder, placing the hammer on one of the steps, and advanced towards her. 'I'm seeing things, aren't I?' he said. 'I don't remember hitting my head.'

His eyes travelled thoroughly from her swept-up hair over the pretty summer dress to the unsuitable sandals, and he shook his head, beginning to smile disbelievingly.

'Do you mind?' Catherine asked. 'You did say to come.'

'Mind? If you're a dream, just don't let me wake up,' he said. 'Not yet.'

He wore only a dusty pair of denim shorts, and he was tanned and sweating slightly on his shoulders and chest. He looked down at himself and grimaced. 'If I'd known you were coming, I'd have cleaned up a bit,' he said. 'I've got a sort of shower arrangement out the back. Make yourself at home and I'll go and wash off some of this dust.'

He swept a pile of clothes off a kitchen chair that stood by a small table near a portable gas stove and small sink bench. 'Sit down,' he invited. His eyes went over her again as she moved into the room, a smile hovering on his mouth. Afraid that she might have given him a wrong impression, she said quickly, 'I don't usually go to the beach dressed like this. It was an impulse. I was supposed to be having lunch in town.'

He nodded, as though the explanation was the most natural in the world. 'I won't be long,' he promised, extracting a clean pair of shorts from the pile of clothing in his arms, and tossing the rest on the bed, before disappearing through a door at the rear of the room.

He came back wearing the clean shorts, his hair darkened with water, and two drink cans in his hands. 'I thought you might be a lemonade girl,' he said, 'but there's beer if you want it.'

'A shandy,' said Catherine. 'if you don't mind.'

'A shandy it is.' He found two glasses and poured straight beer for himself and a mixture of beer and lemonade for her. 'There.' He leaned on the table and smiled down at her as she sipped the refreshing liquid.

'Mm. How do you keep it cold?' she asked.

'There's a little trickle of a stream just up the hill. I have to boil the water for drinking, but it's a good place to keep the drinks cool. Why did you come?'

She looked up at him warily, and then down into her glass. 'You invited me. And I wanted to come.'

'Did you stand up your lunch date?'

'Oh, no. I got stood up. So I was at a loose end, you see. It seemed a good opportunity.'

She smiled at him, her voice deliberately light, but the smile wavered a little as she met his gaze. It was grave, and too knowing.

Then he grinned at her, dispelling the gravity, and lifted his glass to his lips. 'I'm glad,' he said, as he lowered it again. 'Gives me a perfect excuse to take the rest of the day off and entertain my guest.'

'Don't let me stop you!' she protested. 'Can't I hold nails or something?'

'In that outfit?'

'I did bring a bikini.'

'Now that would be too distracting. I'd be hitting my thumb instead of the nails.'

'Next time I'll wear overalls.'

He didn't answer, and there was a tiny silence as she carefully sipped her drink. Her nerves were jumping.

'Do you like canned bean salad?' he asked.

'What? Yes, I think so.'

'I was thinking of opening one for my lunch,' he explained.

'Oh, I'm sorry! I should have brought something——'

'Rot. I don't expect visitors to bring their victuals with them. I've got tomatoes and some tinned lamb tongues, too. Suit you?'

'It sounds lovely. Are you sure you can spare them?'

'Don't worry—I'm well stocked up. And I brought my car. You must have seen it down the track there. If I run out it's only ten minutes to the nearest store. Let's eat, and then I'll take you down to the beach.'

He wouldn't let her help, and she went on drinking her shandy, watching him find plates and open cans, and then slice a couple of tomatoes on to the plates alongside the portions of tongue and salad. He seemed very competent.

As she finished the drink he put one of the plates in front of her and said, 'It might not be up to an Auckland restaurant, but it's all you're getting.'

'Don't apologise. It looks delicious.'

She ate with an appetite that surprised her.

Afterwards, Russel put the dishes into a bowl, and offered a cup of tea which she refused, and a fresh banana which she accepted.

He took the skin from her and disposed of it into a plastic lidded bin under the sink, then straightened up to smile at her. 'Better?' he asked gently.

Catherine avoided his eyes, and said lightly, 'Much, thank you. I hadn't realised how hungry I was.'

After a moment he asked. 'Feel like going down to the beach?'

'Yes, please.'

'We won't swim until our lunch has a chance to settle, but you could put on that bikini now . Shall I go outside?'

She glanced up at him, saw the question in his eyes, and said. 'Thank you. I won't keep you waiting long.'

His mouth quirked with understanding, and he went out, closing the door.

Catherine tucked the towel about her, sarong-style, after changing, and went to join him. 'How do we get down there?' she asked him. 'I had to wear my shoes on your path, because of the stones, but they're hardly suitable for cliff climbing.'

'It isn't exactly a cliff climb, but the path is steep. I'll get you a pair of rubber thongs. They'll be too big for you, but they should help.'

They both laughed when she slid them on. She negotiated the path slowly, clutching at Russel's hand so that he could steady her when her ridiculous footwear threatened to desert her. On the soft sand at last, she shed the thongs with relief, digging her toes into the gritty warmth with a long 'Mmm' of purely sensuous enjoyment as she closed her eyes, lifting her face to the sun and breathing in the salty breeze from the sea.

'You do love it, don't you?' Russel sounded amused, and she opened her eyes and found him watching her with a faint smile, his eyes warm with laughter.

'I told you I do,' she reminded him, looking about her at the broad stretch of sand, the breakers swelling and foaming in deep restless waves. The beach was almost deserted, only a couple of fishermen casting in the distance, and a family group sitting under a large striped umbrella in the other direction.

They walked along the beach side by side, not touching, taking small side excursions to investigate a shell tumbling up on to the sand on the last lick of a wave, a spotted jellyfish quivering glassily on the sand at the tidemark or a heap of glistening seaweed left behind by a receding curve of water. Catherine's hair began to escape in long tendrils from its careful pins, and she pushed it out of her eyes as they walked, while Russel watched, still with that warm laughter in his eyes.

They sat down for a while, half reclining against a soft dune of sand, gazing at the hypnotic beauty of the sea, its blue merging on the horizon with the blue of the sky so that only a faint shimmer betrayed the dividing line.

Catherine drifted sand through her fingers, staring down at her hands, a faint frown emphasising the brooding look on her face. She knew when Russel shifted his eyes from the seascape and the sky, and turned to her instead. She moved, dusting the sand from her fingers, drawing up her knees to wrap her arms about her legs, staring out again to the horizon.

Quietly, Russel said, 'Want to tell me about it?' She stiffened. 'About what?'

'Don't pull wool with me, Cathy. Tell me to

mind my own business if you like. But don't pretend there's nothing wrong. You're all wound up as tight as a clock spring. And you didn't come here just to admire the scenery. You were running.'

Why must he be so damned perceptive? 'I didn't come here to bare my troubles to you,' she said.

'Look, I'm glad you came, no matter why. But you're unhappy, and I'm a friend—aren't I?'

She turned her head and looked at him searchingly. 'Is that what you are, Russ?'

'If that's what you want.'

She dipped her head, running her fingers over the wayward strands that persisted in flying across her face. With a small bitter smile, she said, 'Do you think I need a friend?'

'Looks like it to me. What happened, Cathy?'

She felt sudden tears prick at her eyelids, and shook her head, bewilderedly. 'Nothing, really. It's stupid. My husband and I had a date for lunch. He couldn't make it. That's all. Nothing to make a fuss about.'

'So why are you hurt?'

'Hurt? I don't know if I'm hurt. I was angry—furiously angry. It's so silly. So childish.'

'We're all entitled to be childish now and then. So you had a row over a trivial let-down. Doesn't it happen all the time, in marriages?'

'We didn't have a row. I told him not to worry, not to apologise—he thanked me for understanding. And I put down the phone and I wanted to scream, throw things, break something.'

'Like his neck?'

She grinned faintly. 'Yes. Only he wasn't there.'

'So you came to see me instead. To get your own back?'

She stared at him. 'No!' Then, more uncertainly, trying to be honest, she said, 'No, I don't think so. I just wanted to get away—go somewhere. I remembered you'd be here, and I came. Do you mind?'

'You asked me that before. No, I don't mind. For a lady with so much going for her, you're very insecure, aren't you?'

'Am I? I don't know. Is it insecure to get so upset about a thing like that?'

'Depends. Why were you so upset, do you think?'

'I don't know! I think——' She frowned, concentrating, attempting to analyse her feelings. '—it wasn't just that he had to break our arrangement. It was—it felt like a last straw, and yet I can't think of another instance where the same thing happened—or anything similar. Oh, it must be me! Maybe it's not having the children around—I'm being over-sensitive.'

'Maybe.' Russel sounded enigmatic, almost sceptical. 'And maybe it's a symptom of something deeper. Something that's been going on for a long time.'

'Like what?'

'Like—your unhappiness in your marriage.'

Catherine straightened up, her glance at him knife-sharp. 'There's nothing wrong with my marriage!'

'So you keep telling me. Methinks the lady doth protest too much!' he quoted.

'Do you make a habit of telling married women they're unhappy? Is it a successful line?'

She knew immediately that she had made him blazingly angry. But when he spoke his voice was even. 'Do you really believe that?'

Catherine held on to her own anger a moment

longer. But his eyes met the challenge in hers, and she said, 'I'm sorry, I didn't mean that.'

Russel touched her hand, a gentle, fleeting contact, then leaned back on his hands, watching her. She looked down, digging her fingers into the soft grains of sand. He was right, of course. There had to be some deeper, more long-standing reason for her exaggerated reaction today. But she couldn't discuss it with Russ. She wouldn't answer any more of his disturbing, probing questions.

As if he was aware of her decision, he refrained from asking any more. After a while he asked, 'Ready for a swim?'

She nodded, and pulled off the towel sarong as he stood up and shed his shorts, revealing a skimpy, closefitting garment. He had a trim, lithe body, the sprinkling of masculine hair on it slightly darker than that on his head. He looked good, and she experienced a certain faint satisfaction in the fact. He caught her eye and gave her a slight grin, his eyes laughing knowingly into hers. Suddenly bold, she made a face at him, disparaging the hint of smugness she detected, and he laughed aloud and took her hand to tug her with him as he ran down the beach to the sea.

The first shock was cold, but once they were in deep enough to swim the water rapidly warmed. They were careful not to go out too far, breasting the waves and turning with them to ride into shore, then swimming out again to deeper water. It was exhilarating, and when they finally came out and collapsed side by side, panting, on the towels, Catherine felt tinglingly alive and refreshed. The shadow that had overlaid the day disappeared, and she rolled over on her back and surveyed the blue sky soaring above her with a smile of sheer pleasure.

Russel propped himself on his elbow beside her. 'Good?'

She transferred her smile to him. 'Fantastic!'

His eyes slid over her damp, almost naked body. 'You look gorgeous.'

She felt her face stiffen, and sat up, bending her head to take out the remaining pins. 'My hair's a mess,' she said, shaking down the wet strands over her shoulders so that they shielded her face.

Russel moved so that he was beside her, pushing back the inadequate veil, his fingers brushing her cheek. 'You paid me a compliment the other night. Why can't I pay you one?'

His face bent close to hers, his smile tolerant. She looked at him with a slight effort, and said, 'No reason. Thank you.'

He dropped his hand and watched her trying to smooth her hair. She said, 'I left my comb in the bach.'

'Never mind. It suits you like that.'

Catherine wrung out some of the excess water and pinned her hair up again in a loose, casual knot.

'Bet you didn't bring any sunscreen lotion, did you?' Russel asked.

'Bet *you* didn't either.'

He reached over to his shorts and brought a small plastic bottle out of the pocket. 'You just lost that one,' he said. 'I'll do your back.'

She leaned forward while he stroked the cool lotion on to her skin, lifting the bikini strap momentarily while his fingers trailed underneath it. His touch was pleasant and impersonal, and when he had finished he handed her the bottle and she anointed the rest of her body.

'What about you?' she asked, handing back the lotion.

He smoothed some on his shoulders and chest, but didn't ask her to do his back, and she didn't offer. When she turned on her stomach, resting her head on her arms, he said, 'Want your strap undone?'

'Mm, spose so,' she murmured sleepily, starting to move.

'It's okay,' he said. 'I'll do it for you.'

He was quick and efficient. It was a simple hook, but she wondered at his deftness. He settled back beside her and they lay in silence for a long while, enjoying the warmth, the soft sand, the persistent boom and wash of the sea.

Catherine was half asleep when Russel murmured in her ear, 'We ought to get out of the sun. Feel like another swim?'

She muttered a protest, and he laughed and placed his hand on her nape, the thumb stroking firmly at the groove behind her ear. 'Come on, wake up. You could get sunstroke.'

'Beast!' She began to turn over, remembered her undone strap and was suddenly wide awake as she felt his hand move down her back, caressingly. Then he was hooking the strap together again.

'Come on,' he said. 'Race you to the water.'

He had a head start on her, but he waited at the edge of the waves, and she plunged in and stood waist-deep and used her hands to splash water at him. He came after her, laughing, and picked her up with remarkable ease to throw her in a tangle of arms and legs and loosened hair into the next wave as it foamed towards the shore. She came up with the light of battle in her eyes and managed to duck him once before she found herself held helpless and begging for mercy as he threatened to retaliate. He looked down at her laughing, wriggling and panting in his arms, and she saw his face change and stopped struggling, her heart suddenly lurching, her head jerking back automatically in denial.

It lasted only a moment. Russel said, 'All right, I'll let you off this once,' and let her go, grinning at her as she fell back in the water.

She made a face at him, grateful that he hadn't spoiled it. She liked him so much, and this was fun. Such lovely, innocent fun, nothing to feel guilty about, nothing that she would have to conceal from Jason . . .

There was nothing to be ashamed of. For a moment Russ had been tempted to kiss her—any man would probably have felt the same, with a squirming, scarcely covered young woman held in his arms. She supposed she shouldn't have allowed that horseplay, she wouldn't tempt him again, it wasn't fair . . . She had never had much chance to indulge in that kind of harmless play with a man. She had been so young when she met Jason, there had been no real boy-friends for her before him, and he wasn't a boy, but a man. She had always tried to be adult for him, to meet him on his own level.

They ran back up the beach to collect the towels. Russel wrapped his shorts in his, and went up the path ahead of her, holding her hand and laughing at her efforts to keep up while his thongs slipped wildly about on her wet and sand-dusted feet. At the top she kicked them off, picked them up and ran across the crisp buffalo grass to the bach. He came in behind her and asked, 'Would you like a shower?'

But she was looking at the kitchen clock that stood on the windowsill above the sink, crying in horror, 'Is that the time? I can't I'll have to get dressed. Russ——'

'Okay, I'm going!' He backed out, his hands before him in mock defence.

Catherine threw off the bikini and pulled on her underclothes, hastily dragging on her dress and sliding the zip up as far as she could before rubbing the sand from her feet with the towel, reddening the skin, and thrusting on her sandals. She pulled a comb from her bag and dragged it roughly through the tangles in her hair, leaving it loose because she had lost all the pins by now. She stuffed the towel and bikini into the canvas holdall and opened the door.

Russel was leaning against the porch, turning to smile at her. 'All ready?'

'Yes. I'm sorry I have to rush. I hadn't realised——'

'Will hubby be looking for his dinner?'

'It isn't that. He won't know where I am, and he'll worry.'

'Had a good day?'

'Yes, very. Thank you, Russ.'

'Thank *you*. I enjoyed it, too. Come again.'

Catherine stepped off the little porch, not looking at him, and he caught her arm as she passed him, his grip light but firm. 'No strings,' he said. 'I promise.'

She smiled at him gratefully. 'Maybe I will,' she said. 'But next time you must let me help. I'll work for my dinner.'

'I'll hold you to that.' He released her arm and came beside her, accompanying her down the path. She unlocked the car and slid in, grimacing at the heat that had been locked in all this time. He closed the door and she wound the window down before starting the ignition. Russel stepped back, then leaned forward again and said, 'Don't drive too fast, Cathy. Your husband might worry, but he'll be glad to see you home in one piece.'

'I'll be careful.' The engine turned over, and he stood back again waving as she turned and made off down the sandy road.

She was late, but Jason was, too. He was standing at the door of the house just fitting his key in the lock when she arrived, and he waited while she garaged her car and picked up the holdall and joined him on the doorstep, where he now had the door standing wide.

'Hello,' he said. 'I thought you'd be getting on your glad rags. Sorry I'm late.'

He put his hand on her waist and kissed her briefly, his lips cool and firm. Catherine went ahead of him into the house, feeling his eyes on her as she passed him, very conscious of her salt-dried, still slightly dishevelled hair, and the grains of sand that she could feel between her toes, as well as her total lack of make-up in spite of the elegant dress.

She had her back to him as he closed the door, and then he came behind her and tugged up her zip the couple of inches that she hadn't had time to reach at the bach.

'Thanks,' she said, 'but you needn't bother. I'll be taking it off to have a shower in a minute, anyway.'

'Well, in that case . . .' Jason said insinuatingly, and slid the zip down again, all the way. His hands came about her waist inside the dress, and his lips teased her shoulder. Catherine went rigid, and she felt him still suddenly, noticing. He lifted his head and moved away from her.

'You'd better hurry,' he said. 'I've booked a table for eight o'clock.'

'I think you'd better cancel it,' she said.

'What?'

'I don't think I want to go out tonight, thank you.' Her voice was brittle.

'Look,' said Jason, 'if you're annoyed because of lunch, it's understandable, but don't you think you're being rather silly and childish?'

'Because for once I've failed to fall in with your plans? It may have escaped your notice, but *I've* only just arrived home too. I just don't feel like dashing about in this heat getting ready to go out again in order to salve your guilty conscience. Anyway, I'll have to wash my hair, it's full of sand and sea water. I can't go out with it like this, and by the time it's dry it will be too late.'

'You've been to the beach?'

'Yes, I spent the day on the beach——' She was going to add—*with another man*—because since they had come in she had felt the anger boiling inside her, and she had a sudden desire to hurt him, to show him that although he had let her down, it hadn't been hard to find another male companion. The savagery of her own emotion stopped her, when she realised what she was about to do—use her day with Russel as a cheap weapon in a quarrel with her husband. She wouldn't do that. On all counts it was a mean and vicious tactic.

She didn't say it. Instead she said, 'I'm tired. I'll make us something to eat when I've had a shower.'

But to her surprise, when she came out of the bedroom dressed in a cool cotton caftan, her hair partly blow-dried and pinned back behind her ears, Jason had taken command of the kitchen.

'Sit down,' he said firmly, when she tried to take over. 'You said you're tired, and I'm not helpless.'

He was frying ham steaks, from a pack that had been in the freezer, and he broke two eggs into the pan and added tinned pineapple rings, sliding them on to plates with some leftover potato salad. He put one in front of her and said, 'Wait a minute.'

Bemused, Catherine watched him fetch two long-stemmed glasses and a bottle of white wine. 'You never cook,' she commented, as he put down a glass by her plate and poured wine into it.

'You never let me,' he said mildly. 'I used to cook for myself before I married you. How do you suppose I survived all those years?'

She had supposed that he ate out or from tins, or got girl-friends to cook for him when he was tired of doing that. She knew he had moved out of his parents' home when he was twenty or so. And of course it wasn't true to say he never cooked. When she had been feeling queasy during her pregnancies, he had managed to fend for himself quite often, but she had not seen the results, asking for only dry toast and tea for herself until she felt able to face the sight of food again.

This was the second time today that a man had made a meal for her. It was getting to be a habit, she thought, smiling.

'What do you mean, I never let you?' she asked, as they began to eat.

'I remember you shooting me from the kitchen very firmly when we were first married,' he said, taking a sip of his wine. 'You told me the kitchen was your domain, in no uncertain terms.'

'Did I?' She hadn't remembered that, but she had certainly been eager to prove her prowess as a cook, to impress him with her efficiency as a housewife. She had been anxious to live up to his mother's standards.

'Mind you,' said Jason, 'I have to admit I was glad to let you take over. Cooking isn't my favourite occupation.'

When they had finished the steaks he opened a can of peaches and poured the contents into dishes, topping them with a dollop of ice cream from the freezer. 'Who says I can't cook?' he demanded.

Catherine shook her head, smiling faintly.

As she spooned up the smooth, sweet fruit, he said, 'I really am sorry about the lunch, but it was unavoidable. You see——'

'It's all right,' she said stiffly, 'I'm sure whatever it was, was important.'

'Yes, it was. I want to tell you——'

'Please don't.'

'But Catherine——'

The icy rage was welling again, she would scream, throw something at him. It was impossible, ridiculous, but that was how she felt. She didn't want to know the precise details of the business crisis that had kept him. She had begun to regain her normal calm, she didn't want this tentative peace shattered. She probably wouldn't be able to judge the importance of whatever it was, anyway. Jason's work was very specialised, very complicated, and, as much of it was confidential as well, there were large gaps in her knowledge of what he did.

She looked up at him, and said fiercely, '*I don't want to hear!* Just leave it, *please!*'

His frown was nonplussed. 'All right. I don't understand you——'

She laughed, a brief derision. 'No, you don't.'

Jason pushed away his plate and said, his voice hard. 'What's that supposed to mean?'

'Nothing. I'm sorry, I don't want to start a quarrel. I'm tired.'

Who was she to accuse Jason of not understanding her, anyway? she thought. She didn't even understand herself.

'You've been tired a lot, lately, haven't you?'

She thought she detected some sarcasm in his tone, but when he added, 'You'd better have an early night,' she could see in his expression nothing but a faint weariness. 'I'll get the coffee,' he said, getting up to make it.

He even did the dishes, insisting that he needed no help. He made her sit on the long sofa in the lounge, listlessly watching the television, while he cleaned up the kitchen. Later he joined her, and after a time he pulled her to him with an arm about her shoulders, and began to press light, warm kisses on her temple and cheek, wandering to her mouth. He paused then, his lips touching hers, before he began to part them with an insistent, restless movement of his mouth. Catherine let him do what he wanted, her eyes closed, her body slack against him. His hand on her breast stirred pleasurable sensations, and she let her mouth open a little further under the gentle exploration of his. He moved and picked her up, carrying her to the darkened bedroom, laying her down on the bed.

She stayed there inertly, waiting for him to join her, ready to snuggle into the hard, warm familiarity of his body, to let him gradually overcome the lethargy that held her and build the tiny spark he had started into a passionate blaze. Then she felt his lips feather across her brow, and he pulled the blankets from under her to spread them over her body in the thin caftan. 'Goodnight, my sweet,' she heard him murmur, then the door closed behind him.

She felt slow, hot tears well behind her lids and seep on to the pillow. She lay very still, and when the tears had stopped she drifted into sleep.

CHAPTER FIVE

WHEN next Catherine went to Russel's bach, she was wearing shorts and a plain button-through blouse over her bikini, and sneakers on her feet.

She stopped in the open doorway, looking for him, hearing nothing. She called his name, and when he didn't answer she went in slowly, feeling a little like an intruder, telling herself he wouldn't mind. She put the basket she was carrying on the little table, and looked about. The sawhorse was still there, and the smell of new wood, but the lining was finished. She wandered out to the doorway again, saw that Russel had begun building the deck, not far off the ground, resting on thick four-by-two joists, a few planks already nailed into position. It would be sunny, but in the afternoon one of the scraggy kanukas would shade it, its small aromatic leaves making a pattern of light and shade on the boards, and it had a great view of the sea.

As she stood there he appeared suddenly from the cliff path, his skin glistening with drops of salt water, his hair sleek and damp.

'Cathy!' he exclaimed, and came towards her, breathing a little hard. 'I thought I heard something—have you been here long?'

He was smiling, and she smiled back, glad because he seemed glad to see her. 'I've just arrived,' she told him. 'You're shirking.'

He put a wet arm about her, guiding her into the house.

'Smoke time,' he said. 'Give me a break. I've been working since six this morning.'

'I take it back.' Catherine laughed as he dropped his arm and went to pick up his shorts from the camp bed. 'I can see you've been making progress. It looks good.'

He glanced around. 'A coat of paint next,' he told her. 'I've done the ceiling.' He grimaced and held his neck, groaning in reminiscence. 'You any good with a paintbrush?'

'I haven't had much experience,' she admitted. 'But I've come to work, this time.'

On his way to the rear door, he grinned at her. 'I'll keep you to that. Won't be long.'

He didn't give her a paintbrush, but a foam plastic roller, a shallow tin dish and some ice blue vinyl paint. He left her to use them while he returned to nailing planks on to the deck outside. She soon got the feel of it, and enjoyed making long sweeps with the roller, seeing the paint flow on thick and bubbly, then gradually smoothing as she went over it, spreading the colour until it covered the greyish wallboard in a thin coat.

'Is it all right?' she asked Russel apprehensively when he came in and stood surveying the two and a half walls she had done.

He seemed surprised at her uncertainty. 'Terrific,' he assured her. 'One more coat and it'll be perfect.'

'*Another one?*' Catherine moaned in mock dismay.

'This stuff dries very fast,' he said solemnly, and they both laughed.

Russel said, 'I'll get us something to eat.'

'No,' she said. 'I brought food with me.'

He watched as she lifted the folded towel from the top of the basket on the table, and removed the clean tea-towel beneath it, revealing a whole cold roasted chicken, bread rolls, a lettuce, boiled eggs and tomatoes. And lying on the bottom with an ice pad, a bottle of white wine.

He was bending close now, looking, smiling. 'Hey, that's great! I'm suddenly starving. Let's take it outside, away from this paint smell.'

They ate on the half-finished deck, leaning against the wall of the house, their legs stretched out before them. Afterwards they sat talking for a while until Catherine packed the leftovers up and took them inside, and when she had finished the walls she went out to help him while the paint dried.

He nailed on the last plank, and subsided, panting theatrically, on the new deck. 'A cold drink, and then a swim,' he decreed. 'We deserve it.'

They dived into the surf together, and this time Catherine was careful to avoid teasing him. As they lay on the sand later, he touched a finger to a wavy white line on her thigh, just below the bikini pants. 'What's that?'

She shifted quickly, and he took his hand away. 'A stretch mark,' she said. 'I don't have many, but——'

'From having babies?'

'Yes.'

'You're so slim, I can hardly believe it. You don't have any marks on your tummy.'

She moved again, restlessly, under his inspection. 'Stop it, Russ! You're embarrassing me.'

'I'm sorry,' he said. 'I didn't mean to.'

His apology was so sincere, she stopped being embarrassed and smiled at him.

'What's it like, having children?' he asked her.

'You mean—what's it like having them—or *having* them?'

He laughed, and settled himself on one elbow to

look at her face. 'No, I mean, how does it feel to be a parent? I fancy myself as a father, some day. I like kids.'

He'd be a good father, too, she thought. He'd be a lot of fun, and kind with it. 'I haven't really thought about it,' she said, 'not to the extent of putting it into words. It just happens. And it's wonderful but scary too.'

'Scary?' he queried.

'They're so small, at first—for a long time really. Even now, sending them off to Australia like that, they seemed so small, such babies, to be making the trip alone. And they depend on me for so much, love, security, everything.'

'Not on you alone, surely?'

'No, of course there's Jason, too. But I'm their *mother*.'

Russel looked at her curiously. 'He's their father, isn't he?'

'He's a very good father. Only he doesn't have a lot of time. And being a father isn't a full-time job.'

'But being a mother is?'

'Until they go to school, anyway.'

'Yours are at school now. So what are you going to do with the rest of your time?'

'I don't know. I guess I could serve on a few more committees. There are plenty of charities wanting voluntary workers.'

'But that isn't what you want.'

'Maybe I'm too selfish.'

'You've spent six years of your life taking care of a couple of fairly helpless, fairly demanding little human beings. I don't think it's selfish if you feel like doing something just for your own sake, for a change.'

A quick flare of excitement, a sense of

adventure, flickered and died. 'The trouble is, I don't know what I want to do,' she said ruefully. 'If I had a specific talent, a career that I'd interrupted for marriage, an ambition—but I don't. Just a feeling that there ought to be more to life—to *me*.'

'There isn't anything missing in you.'

'Oh, yes, there is! Sometimes I wonder if I'm me at all. If there *is* a me.'

'What do you mean?'

'Nothing.' Catherine laughed softly at herself, embarrassed all over again, wanting to pretend she hadn't said it.

But Russel persisted. 'What do you mean? How can you feel that way? As though you don't exist.'

'But I don't,' she explained. 'Not as a person in my own right. I'm the original nobody. Somebody's daughter, then somebody's wife, now somebody's mother. Nobody on my own. Nobody who's ever done anything worthwhile or interesting.'

He frowned, trying to understand. 'The world is full of nobodies,' he said. 'Little faceless people who never make the news. But that doesn't make them unimportant—non-existent. Do you want to be famous?'

'No. Just—effective. Someone who does things, someone who isn't just an extension of other people, living their lives.'

'You mean, you want a life of your own?'

'Oh, it's a cliché, isn't it?' she sighed. 'No, that isn't what I mean, exactly. But I can—relate to that. I'd like to be my own person. That's a cliché, too, isn't it?'

'Are you a feminist?'

'Not really. At least, not actively. Yes, intellectually, for equal rights and all that. But I don't think that women can dodge the differences, pretend they aren't there, ask doctors to aid and abet when they decide that being a woman is—inconvenient. Being a mother is full of inconveniences, but that's what it's all about, isn't it? Being female. Denying it is cheating, pretending to be *like* men, not just equal to them.'

'Do you mean every woman should be a mother?'

'Oh, no. No. But I think the ones who are can't just abdicate. It's like—well, you wouldn't know it, but when a woman is having a baby—I mean, in the actual process, there's a time when suddenly you can't go through with it, you want out, *now*. And you know that's impossible, that there's no way out. You're in it now, and nothing you do is going to change things. You can't stop anything any more. Because it's done, it's too late. And marriage, having a family, it's——'

'It's like that?' Russel asked quietly.

'Not in the same say. And it isn't anything to do with not loving them—husband, children. It's just that you're in there now, and there's no way out ... Not without destroying so much, hurting them, hurting yourself.'

'Do you want out?'

'No, I don't. I really don't. I just want—more. Greedy. Wanting to have my cake and eat it, perhaps. Irresponsible. I'm not making sense,' she added quickly, apologetically. 'It's just a mood. Don't take any notice of me.'

She got up and ran back into the water, ashamed of her confidences, her muddled feelings.

Later she showered in Russel's primitive bathroom, the water cool and fresh, and combed out her wet hair before pinning it up.

'Mrs Clyde,' he said, when she emerged into the other room.

Her lids came down over her eyes as she crossed the bare floor to pick up the basket and put her rolled towel in it, the wet bikini wrapped inside.

She made a task of it, tucking in the loose end of the towel, straightening the wrinkles. And then Russel was standing behind her, his hands on her shoulders turning her to face him. 'I didn't mean to hurt you,' he said. 'I wouldn't.'

'I know.'

'Cathy.' His voice was soft.

But she wasn't Cathy. She was Mrs Clyde, wife and mother. Quietly she said, 'Please don't, Russ. It's been such a lovely day.'

He smiled faintly, ruefully, and dropped his hands.

This time he didn't accompany her down the path, but stood on the new deck and watched her until she was out of his sight behind the tall flax.

Russel came to the first night of the pantomime by special invitation of the producer. Bridie was flushed with success at the end of it, for the patients had certainly made no secret of their appreciation. But Russel's approval sealed the evening for her. He seemed genuinely impressed, his praise sincere and not overdone.

He turned to Catherine as Bridie rushed off to help a squirming child get out of a ladybird costume without wrecking it. 'You look ethereal,' he said. 'As though you might vanish any moment.'

'I won't do that,' she promised. 'It's the dress.'

It was chiffon, pale blue, and she supposed, since he had bought paint that colour for his bach, he must like it. She had taken off the cleverly fashioned wings of cellophane and wire for fear of damaging them. But the dress had been adapted from an old evening frock, and was not as fragile as it appeared.

'I like it,' Russel said warmly. 'And you can act, too.'

'Thank you. Perhaps I could make a career of it.'

'Would you like to?'

She laughed a little, not imagining he was serious. One of the cast came up to speak to them, and soon afterwards Catherine went off to the makeshift dressing room to change.

Jason had waited up for her this time. When she came into the lounge where he sat with a book, he put it down and smiled at her and asked, 'How did it go?'

'Very well, I think. Bridie's pleased, and the patients loved it.'

'Good. Feel like going away for a few days?'

They had discussed it before, concluding that between tonight and a last rehearsal before the second performance of the pantomime didn't give them enough time to make a holiday worthwhile. They had decided that being at home without the children was sufficient break for them.

But Catherine thought she knew why Jason was suggesting a last-minute change of plan. Christmas Day had been flat without the children, and although they had exchanged presents and enjoyed the luxury of lying in, ending the day with dinner and dancing among a crowd of strangers at a city night spot, her mood had been inescapably depressed. Even at dinner, she had sat across the table from him feeling tense and tongue-tied, almost as though he was a stranger instead of her husband. It had been the same the day they had met for their postponed lunch, two people sharing a table who apparently had little to say to each other. Jason had seemed preoccupied, and she had almost immediately begun to feel that he would rather have been back in his office, that he was only lunching with her from a sense of obligation, humouring her because he had promised and he wouldn't go back on a promise. When he spoke to her she answered him stiffly, her eyes wandering over the other people in the room, not meeting his. It had not been a success.

But the thought of going away was immediately attractive, even though it could only be for a short while. The house seemed empty without the children, the unnatural silence almost oppressive. And perhaps if they moved to a different environment for a little while, she and Jason would lose some of the odd constraint that seemed to be growing between them.

'Can we?' she asked eagerly. 'It's a bit late to try and book anything, surely?'

'We should find somewhere, if we're not too choosy about where we go. Any preferences?'

'I don't mind.'

'I'll phone some places in the morning, see what I can do.'

He did, starting early, and eventually was able to tell her he had struck it lucky. 'A cancellation at Paihia,' he told her. 'How do you fancy a visit to the Bay of Islands?'

It sounded good, and very fortunate at this time of year.

The North, the 'winterless' North, with its unspoiled beaches, its remnants of the great forests which had once covered the land, its calm waterways and its sense of history, drew them into its heart as they drove later in the day towards the

Bay. Here scattered islands dreaming on azure waters shot with purple and green and deep indigo echoed its name. Here the European history of New Zeland had its origins, for after Captain Cook's circumnavigation of these southern islands, the sealers and whalers who plundered the Pacific had found the bay a useful port of call, where they could refurbish their battered ships after long journeys before heading homeward, gather fresh spars for masts from the tall kauri forests, and barter with the local Maoris for supplies of food.

Later the notorious town of Kororareka had catered for the less respectable needs of sailors who had sometimes spent years at sea under brutally strict discipline and in cramped and unhealthy conditions. At one time it was said that every house on the foreshore was a grogshop selling cheap, often poisonous rum. And at the Mission station at Paihia across the water, the good men of the cloth and their intrepid British wives had wrung their hands in dismay and horror when their Maori protégés were enticed into the sailors' arms with the promise of a red calico dress and a string of glass beads.

That history was difficult to credit now, Catherine thought, as, on the day after their arrival at the thriving town of Paihia, they took a ferry to cross over the harbour. Kororareka had long since shed its name and was now called Russell for Lord John Russell, an eminently respectable nineteenth-century Colonial Secretary. And Russell was a quiet little town, its early history carefully preserved in its small museum and its remaining historic buildings.

Those few short days were filled with sunshine and history as they solemnly examined the bullet holes in the little white wooden church that

remained from a famous engagement between
Maoris and settlers after the town had achieved
respectability as the temporary capital of the new
nation; climbed Flagstaff Hill to view the
breathtaking beauty of the bay and read the
plaque commemorating the raising of the staff to
symbolise the unity of the two races after a stormy
history when the hostile chief Hone Heke had four
times chopped down its predecessors in defiance of
British authority; and wandered through the
beautiful interior and gardens of the 'Treaty
House' at Waitangi where the historic treaty
between Maori and Pakeha, giving sovereignty to
Queen Victoria, had been signed.

They took a cruise about the harbour and past
some of the famous islands, viewed the Hole in the
Rock, a great natural archway rearing from the
water, large enough for tourist launches to go
through, and saw dolphins cavorting in the wake
of the boat, leaping in graceful curves from the sea
behind them, grinning as they came up alongside,
apparently hugely enjoying themselves.

And at night they made love in their motel
room, locking out the world and history and
daytime.

Catherine felt more relaxed and happy than she
had for a long time, and Jason was always a
considerate and gentle lover. The nights were
warm and sea-scented, and they could sleep in the
mornings until the sun woke them with its
impatient heat. There was no office to claim Jason,
and no children clamoured for Catherine's attention. For the first time since the children had left,
she ceased to miss them.

CHAPTER SIX

A FEW days after their return, with Jason back at work again, Catherine answered the phone to find that Russel was on the line. She wasn't really surprised.

'I want to talk to you,' he said. 'Can you make lunch?'

'What about?' she enquired, and was intrigued when he answered, with laughter in his voice, 'Business. I'll tell you about it over lunch.'

When they met she scanned his face with anxious curiosity, but he teased her by insisting on eating first, and only over coffee he looked at her, his eyes smiling at her impatience, and said, 'You'd like to have a job, wouldn't you?'

'What are you suggesting?'

He grimaced. 'Don't be like that.' His eyes were wicked, and Catherine stifled laughter and said, 'Stop it! What are you really getting at?'

'I have a new show to produce. I want you in it.'

'Me? *Why?*'

'Because I think you'd be good at it. You needn't look so wary. This is no casting couch.'

'I wasn't——'

'You were wondering what the angle is. Don't bother to deny it.'

'Russel, will you please get to the point?'

'I just did. I've got an interesting assignment. It's a programme for kids—not toddlers, the slightly older ones, say six to twelve. I want it to be lively and unpredictable and very watchable. And it needs a front person, someone who can talk to kids without patronising them—there'll be a bunch of them in the studio—and someone who can come across as natural and fun to be with.'

'Me?' Catherine said again, doubtfully.

'I've seen you with the kids in that hospital. You're good with them, warm and friendly and funny. And you could write some of your own material, the fill-in bits. I want to make it your show, build it around your personality. One of the problems, I think, with some of the children's television chat-and-link formats is that the anchor people are interchangeable—clones.'

Catherine laughed. 'I'm flattered you don't see me as a clone.'

Russel didn't laugh with her. For a moment he looked deadly serious. Then he said, 'Will you do it?'

'I'm an amateur,' she protested. 'Surely there must be any number of professional actresses——'

'The good ones are over-exposed. I want a new face, a fresh talent.'

'Talent?'

He suddenly leaned over and took her hand in a firm grip. 'Stop doubting yourself. You're a beautiful young woman, and you can act—so you're not Bernhardt, who is? You have the particular qualities I need to get this show off the ground. I want you!' He grinned. 'And you want a career, something to make you feel a person again.'

She shook her head. 'You're taking advantage. I talk too much.'

'Are you saying no?'

'I'd like some time to think about it.'

'Will you have to ask your husband's permission?'

'No.' She stared at him. 'But of course I'll have to consult him.'

'Will you?' Without waiting for her reply, he said, 'Yes, I suppose you will. Don't let him talk you out of it, Cathy—please!'

She didn't answer him, staring down at the empty cup in front of her. 'Surely you can't just give me the job, like that?'

'Not quite. I'll need to see how you go in front of the cameras, of course, but I'm sure you'll be fine.'

'You're so confident,' she murmured.

'I know you'll be terrific. I know it.'

Catherine half-smiled, shaking her head again.

'Trust me, I do know what I'm doing,' he assured her.

Some of his enthusiastic confidence transferred itself to her. She said, suddenly reckless, 'I won't tell Jason yet. Let's do whatever tests you need first. I—I'll make it a surprise.'

The tilt of his head was faintly sardonic, but he said nothing except, 'Good girl! I'll take you to the studio now, if it's okay?'

When he took her into the building she was taken aback at the vast barnlike space in which the sets were placed. Each set gave the illusion of an enclosed room which was produced by three walls and some furniture, but when she was seated and asked to 'Be natural' while a total stranger asked her questions, she found it difficult to ignore the cameras and lights.

When they played the videotape back later, she was relieved at how natural she seemed, the nervousness hardly showing at all.

Russel was quietly triumphant. He didn't say, 'I told you so,' but his smile and the teasing light in his eyes said it for him.

Not until it was officially confirmed that the job was hers did she tell Jason about it. She knew she had surprised him, although he showed it only in a slight lifting of his dark brows, and a listening stillness while she told him about it.

'I didn't know you'd applied for the job,' he said when she had finished.

'I didn't exactly apply.' She hesitated.

'Well? How did you come to get it, then?'

It was a reasonable question. 'Through a friend,' she said. 'Russel Thurston is the producer—you remember, he helped us with the hospital pantomime.'

'Yes, I remember,' Jason said slowly. 'He's a friend?'

'Well—yes. I've met him a few times since. He's nice,' she finished almost defiantly.

Jason's lids hid his eyes. Sounding rather bored, he said, 'I see. Well, good luck in your new career. When shall I see you on television?'

'I'm not sure yet. Jason, you don't mind, do you?'

He looked at her steadily. 'Are you asking my permission?'

Her brows came together. 'Not really. I—I would like your—approval, though.'

'You have it. If it will make you happy, go ahead with my blessing. It might be interesting having a TV star for a wife. Only don't forget the children will be home in a couple of weeks.'

'I hadn't forgotten,' she said thinly. She didn't know why, but somehow his reaction had produced a slight chill in her heart.

The children didn't come home after all as planned. A telegram arrived from Australia saying that Michael had chickenpox, just the day before they were due to leave. By this time Catherine was in a whirlwind of preparation for the programme, consulting with Russel, learning camera techniques and helping to write the script for the first filming. The programme was to be a regular one, screened three times a week, and she had quickly discovered that Russel was a perfectionist. She came up against a new aspect of his personality altogether when she phoned and told him she was needed in Australia.

'What are you talking about?' he asked, sounding blankly amazed.

'It's Michael,' she explained. 'He's sick. And Jenny will probably get it, too.'

'Get what?'

'Chickenpox.'

There was an expressive silence. Then Russel said quietly, 'Cathy, you're not thinking straight. You can't fly to Australia just like that. We're taping your first show next week.'

'But the children——' she faltered weakly.

'Chickenpox, you said. It isn't a matter of life and death, is it?'

'No, but—Russ, they're only little.'

'They won't be little for ever, and in the meantime you'll have passed up the chance of having a career that will mean something to you after they've grown up.'

'That's looking a long way ahead.'

'Maybe. I thought you really wanted to do this show.'

'I do. But——'

'Listen to me, Cathy. You'll never get another chance, if you cancel out now. We've got everything ready to go, and I don't know how we'd get anyone as good at short notice. Some of the material we're using is yours, you wrote it yourself. It's tailor-made. You throw that all up, and you're finished as far as TV goes. Is that what you want to do?'

He waited, while she twisted the cord of the telephone in her hand and thought of Michael and Jenny, miserable and missing her, and then of all the work and time and money that had already gone into the programme. Almost sulkily, she said, 'If I was sick, you'd have to find a replacement, wouldn't you?'

'You're not sick.' He had never sounded so cold to her before.

But my child is, she thought. *He's sick and he's needing me.*

But did he? Althea would cosset him, and Jenny too, if she contracted the illness. They would be well looked after. No worries there. Her maternal instincts had been running haywire. Her world steadied as she took a breath and said, 'Russel, I'm sorry. I'm being ridiculous. Of course I'll stay.'

'Not ridiculous,' he said gently. 'Just a mother. Got things in proportion now?'

'I think so. I still feel guilty, though.'

'Wouldn't you have felt guilty if you'd gone?'

'Yes,' she admitted, 'I suppose I would.'

'Grin and bear it,' he said. 'I'm sorry, Cathy.'

She put down the receiver with an odd sense of having crossed a bridge and burned it behind her. But there was another one yet to come.

Jason, when he read the telegram, simply asked, 'Have you booked a flight?'

'I'm not going,' she told him.

'What?' He looked up from the slip of paper and stared hard at her.

'I'm not going over there,' she said. 'I'm sure your mother can cope perfectly well. She hasn't asked me to come.'

'No, but——' It was the first time she could remember seeing him at a loss for words.

'It's only chickenpox,' Catherine said defensively. 'Nothing serious. By the time I got there it could be virtually all over.'

'Rot! It's a couple of hours by air.'

She bit her lip, her voice rising in spite of the effort she made to keep it level and calm. 'Well, I'm not going. I have to start filming next week, and I can't go!'

'Can't?' His voice was hard.

'I *can't*!' she reiterated. 'I have a contract.'

Russel had not reminded her of that, she had only just remembered it herself. Fleetingly, she was grateful to him for not holding it over her head. 'I can't just walk out on it.'

Jason was frowning, his mouth thin. 'All right,' he said, 'I suppose you can't. Have you contacted my parents?'

'No. I suppose we could phone, couldn't we?'

She wanted to speak to the children, reassure them, tell them herself why she couldn't come over and be with them.

'Yes, we could,' Jason agreed. But he sounded abstracted, and his eyes on her were hard and assessing, as though he couldn't quite make her out, as though he had found something in her which he had never suspected, and didn't much like.

It wasn't easy to explain to the children, of course, and their voices sounded forlorn over the wire, though the prospect of seeing their mother on TV when they were home generated some mild excitement. All the same, when the phone call was over, Catherine found her eyelashes were wet.

Jason looked grim as he watched her brush the tears with a fingertip. For a moment she thought he was going to move towards her, perhaps hold her in comforting arms. But he swung away from her instead, and went to switch on the television set for the news.

While she was working, she was concentrating too much for the children's welfare to bother her more than peripherally, the challenge of learning new skills and taking part in a totally new activity enough to keep her from fretting about the progress of their illness. In due course Althea reported that, as expected, Jenny had developed spots, too. She also said that both invalids were as happy as could be expected, but reading between the lines of the blue airletter, Catherine morbidly detected a hint of disapproval of her own inaction.

She sensed disapproval from Jason, too, and her own mood became increasingly brittle. She felt continually on the defensive, and was shocked and bothered by the edginess that seemed to have crept into her relationship with Jason.

She knew that the sharp little exchanges were consequent on strain, and that she was as much to blame as Jason, but it did seem that he was showing uncharacteristic bursts of temper. One evening when she came back at him with a snap over some charged remark, he returned rather savagely, 'If this is what going to work does for you, you'd better give it up!'

Catherine's heart actually lurched at the thought. 'You don't like it, do you?' she challenged him. 'Why didn't you say so when I asked you, instead of pretending to approve?'

'You're talking nonsense,' he said impatiently. 'You didn't exactly ask for my permission!'

'Should I have? Is that what rankles, Jason? That I didn't request your permission, like a good, obedient little wife?'

'Stop trying to pick a fight,' he said wearily. 'You'd better go to bed.'

'I'm not tired! And you can't send me to bed like one of the children.'

His mouth thinned, and something in his eyes made her suddenly remember vividly that last night, when he had reached for her in their bed, she had said she was tired—last night and a good many nights recently.

She felt the flush on her cheeks, and started back as he came towards her, his step deliberate. 'Can't I?' he said softly.

'Jason, don't——'

He swung her up into his arms, his grip strong and unbreakable, and she was too surprised and also too dismayed by his unexpected behaviour, to struggle much.

He strode into the bedroom and flung her down on the bed, and even as she made to struggle up, he sat on the side of it and hauled her into his arms, bending her head back with his kiss. She fought for breath, because his mouth was suffocating, pressing her lips against her closed teeth until she was forced, moaning, to open them to his implacable invasion. His mouth lifted abruptly and his arms slackened, and he said gratingly, with a hard mockery, 'I'm glad you're not tired tonight.'

Furious and frightened, Catherine jerked one arm free and swung her palm with all her strength against his cheek.

The sharp, vicious sound seemed to echo in the quiet room. She heard his breath pulled in harshly, and her own light, quick breathing.

For a moment she felt his hands tight on her shoulders, as though he wanted to shake her—or break her. Then he stood up, thrusting her roughly back against the pillows, and stalked out of the room.

While she lay there she heard the back door slam, and then silence. It was hours before Jason came back, and then he undressed and lay unmoving beside her in the darkness, while she pretended to be sleeping.

Increasingly, Catherine was grateful for having her work, and longed for the children to return home. Then she felt guilty and bewildered, because both were a buffer between her and Jason. That was appalling, signifying something badly wrong in their marriage. There must be something she should do about that, but Jason was uncompromisingly aloof and sarcastic, and she found herself either tongue-tied or reacting with barbed, defensive remarks when they were together.

At night she lay tensely beside him in the double bed until exhaustion overcame her at last and she slept. She didn't think that Jason was sleeping much, either.

Once, he turned and touched her arm, and she stiffened involuntarily, her breath catching in her throat in some kind of anticipation. After a moment he removed his hand and lay on his back. She knew that he was staring into the darkness, thinking. Her throat worked, she tried to force herself to make some move towards him, something to help heal the frightening gulf between them. But a hard knot of anger and resentment, its causes obscure and multiple, seemed to have built up inside her. She didn't move.

Althea wrote that the children were well enough to travel, and that she and Winston had decided to accompany them back to New Zealand. '. . . *hoping it's not presuming too much to expect a welcome from you both,'* she had written. *'We shan't stay long, but Jenny, in particular, is still pulled down by the illness, and as you, Catherine dear, are working now, I feel it would be a good idea for us to spend a few weeks with you.'*

Althea organising again. Catherine's heart sank, even as she wrote a carefully grateful reply in appreciation of her mother-in-law's thoughtfulness, containing an invitation to stay as long as they liked.

It was odd seeing the children again after so long. They both looked taller and older, and she felt the threat of foolish tears as she hugged them under Althea's and Winston's indulgent eyes.

They were both a little pale, and still sported a couple of tiny scars each from the chickenpox. Jenny was sensitive about one on her forehead, and Althea had cut her hair into a fringe to hide it.

'I knew you wouldn't mind,' Althea told Catherine as she explained it in an undertone, while the children were helping Winston and Jason collect the luggage.

'Of course not,' Catherine said automatically. 'It was very wise of you. Thank you.' But Jenny looked different, and the difference produced a peculiar little ache in her throat. She was assailed by a sudden wave of the guilt that she thought she had conquered weeks ago, a conviction that, no matter what, she should have moved heaven and earth to be with Jenny and Michael when they were ill.

Back at the house, the children's excitement covered any strain among the adults, and Catherine let them have their heads and stay up late, until a difference of opinion became a quarrel, and Jenny burst into tears.

Catherine made to take the child in her arms,

but she had run to her grandmother, and Althea was gathering her up, saying, 'There, my lamb, you're just tired, that's all. You should have been in bed ages ago.'

She hadn't looked at Catherine, but Catherine felt the sting of implied criticism, and said quickly, standing up, 'Come on, you two, into bed. You can sleep in tomorrow, and the next day you'll be back at school.'

When she had seen them into bed, Althea came to kiss them goodnight, and as the two women returned to the lounge together, she said, 'Catherine dear, do you think it wise to send them to school so soon? Jenny still looks very peaky, and Michael had a bad dose, you know.'

'I know. But they've missed two weeks already of the term. I think they should go back very soon.'

'Well, if you and Jason both think so . . .'

Catherine flushed slightly. She hadn't discussed it with Jason. They had discussed very few things lately. Anyway, he had always left most decisions regarding the children to her.

Althea was saying delicately, 'If it's a question of taking care of them in the daytime while you work, my dear, remember that Winston and I will be here to look after them.'

Catherine took a moment to swallow down a quick rush of anger. 'It isn't that,' she said evenly. 'I'm grateful for the offer, of course, but if I'm working while they are at home, I can always get a babysitter. I certainly wouldn't send them to school if I thought they were too unwell to go.'

'No, of course not. I didn't mean to suggest— forgive me, dear.'

Oh, didn't you? Catherine thought grimly. Aloud she said, 'Of course. Shall we make some more coffee? I'm sure the men would like some.'

'Yes, in some things Jason *is* like his father,' Althea said. 'Coffee at any time, day or night. Not that I would say no to a cup myself, just at the moment. Flying makes me thirsty.'

That first evening was easy, compared to the days and evenings that followed. Catherine felt the strain of presenting the picture of a happy and thriving marriage to Jason's parents, and of withstanding Althea's steely gentility when the older woman felt duty bound to advise her on her handling of the children. She needed extra reserves of patience, too, to cope with Jenny's new fractiousness. It was unfair, she told herself, to blame Althea for that. She was genuinely grateful for Althea's devoted nursing during the chickenpox, but she couldn't help wishing that she would not give in to every whim of Jenny's with quite such eagerness. With Michael, his grandparents were considerably more hard-headed, apparently believing that boys should be turned into little men early in life, but that only compounded the problem. Michael took out his jealousy on his sister, and Jenny was fast developing into a little minx, twisting the adults around her finger, and smirking at her brother behind their backs.

Perhaps, Catherine reminded herself, Jenny represented the daughter that Althea had never had. She had gathered that Winston had had a large hand in the upbringing of Jason, and Althea was compensating herself with the second generation. It was understandable, but it didn't make the situation much easier to live with.

Catherine's nerves became frayed, and early one evening after an exchange of carefully worded opinion with Althea, she went into the bedroom, closing the door with a snap to lean back against it, eyes closed, while she drew a deep breath and let it out in a long sigh of frustration.

'Something wrong?' Jason's voice brought her eyes open, and she saw him standing by the long wardrobe, his lean, muscled torso bare as he held a shirt he had just pulled from a hanger.

'What are you doing in here?' she asked. She had thought he was in the garden outside, talking to his father.

His eyes glittered. 'It happens to be my room as well,' he reminded her sarcastically. 'If it pleases you, I can move into the guest room when my parents have gone. Meantime, I'm afraid you'll have to put up with my presence.'

He hauled on the shirt, pushing it into his pants with angry movements, and beginning to fasten the buttons.

She hadn't meant that at all, but the sarcasm stung, and she flashed back, 'When are they going? I'd like to know.'

'Can't wait?' he asked nastily. 'Okay, darling, you can ask them to leave whenever you like.'

'You know I can't do that.'

'Do you want *me* to?'

'No. I'm—grateful for all they've done. It's just that I find it—difficult to deal with your mother's advice.'

'Yes, you always resented anyone else having a say in what happens with the children, didn't you? Even me.'

'That isn't true!' she objected.

'Isn't it?' He slanted her an indifferent glance, pulling a tie from the rack on the wardrobe door and quickly knotting it about his neck. He shrugged. 'Is this straight?'

Once Catherine would have walked over and tugged it straight for him, whether it needed it or

Say Hello to Yesterday

Holly Weston had done it all alone.

She had raised her small son and worked her way up to features writer for a major newspaper. Still the bitterness of the the past seven years lingered.

She had been very young when she married Nick Falconer—but old enough to lose her heart completely when he left. Despite her success in her new life, her old one haunted her.

But it was over and done with—until an assignment in Greece brought her face to face with Nick, and all she was trying to forget. . . .

Time of the Temptres

The game must be played his way!

Rebellion against a cushioned, controlled life had landed Eve Tarrant in Africa. Now only the tough mercenary Wade O'Mara stood between her and possible death in the wild, revolution-torr jungle.

But the real danger was Wade himself—he had made Eve aware of herself as a woman.

"I saved your neck, so you feel you owe me something," Wade said. "But you don't owe me a thing, Eve. Get away from me." She knew she could make him lose his head if she tried. But that wouldn't solve anything. . . .

Your Romantic Adventure Starts Here.

Born Out of Love

It had to be coincidence!

Charlotte stared at the man through a mist of confusion. It was Logan. An older Logan, of course, but unmistakably the man who had ravaged her emotions and then abandoned her all those years ago.

She ought to feel angry. She ought to feel resentful and cheated. Instead, she was apprehensive—terrified at the complications he could create.

"We are not through, Charlotte," he told her flatly. "I sometimes think we haven't even begun."

Man's World

Kate was finished with love for good.

Kate's new boss, features editor Eliot Holman, might have devas tating charms—but Kate couldn' care less, even if it was obvious that he was interested in her.

Everyone, including Eliot, thoug Kate was grieving over the loss c her husband, Toby. She kept it a carefully guarded secret just how cruelly Toby had treated her and how terrified she was of trusting men again.

But Eliot refused to leave her alone, which only served to infu ate her. He was no different from any other man. . . or was he?

These FOUR free Harlequin Presents novels allow you to enter the world of romance, love and desire. As a member of the Harlequin Home Subscription Plan, you can continue to experience all the moods of love. You'll be inspired by moments so real...so moving...you won't want them to end. So start your own Harlequin Presents adventure by returning the reply card below. <u>DO IT TODAY!</u>

not. Now she said woodenly, 'Yes. Where are you going?'

'I've got a meeting tonight—I told you.'

'Oh. I'd forgotten. Will you be late?'

It was an automatic query. She was unprepared for the cynicism of his glance at her as he said, 'What difference does it make to you? If you're not asleep when I come in, you'll be giving a good imitation.'

He picked up his jacket from the bed, and she moved aside as he came towards the door. For a moment Jason hesitated with his fingers about the handle, and looked down at her.

She thought he was going to kiss her, and stayed still, looking back at him with faint trepidation, her heart beating heavily.

The moment stretched between them, the tension building, then something flickered in his eyes, and she saw his face change, his mouth curve into bitterness. He made an almost inaudible, impatient sound and wrenched at the door, leaving it swinging open as he left.

CHAPTER SEVEN

IN spite of Althea's disapproval of their return to school, the children had shown no ill effects and were quite happy. The first few programmes had been shown on television, and they were intrigued at watching their mother speaking to them from the screen. At school it had given them the status of minor celebrities.

The programme went out live three times a week, but segments of it 'were videotaped beforehand, so that Catherine was actually working about twenty-four hours each week. At first most of the film excerpts were of interviews with people that might reasonably interest the young viewers—a writer of children's adventure stories, a zoo-keeper, a famous racing driver—and with children who had unusual stories of their own to tell. Catherine wondered where the research team found all the material that they did. One day she talked to a little girl who had survived, with a group of adults, the wreck of her father's yacht off the Fiji islands, and however frightening the incident might have been at the time, the child in retrospect seemed to find it both thrilling and almost enjoyable. Another child who impressed her was suffering from several physical disabilities, yet still managed to take part in a number of activities such as horseriding, swimming and archery. Her experience in hospital visiting enabled Catherine to conduct the interview naturally and without embarrassment to either of them.

She still made the hospital visits, too, and found

that her presence was doubly appreciated by the young patients who had seen her TV programme. Sometimes she was asked for an autograph, and Bridie teased her about 'the price of fame'.

'You're looking a bit strained, though,' she added, her gaze shrewdly knowledgeable. 'I know you're enjoying the job, but are you sure you're not taking on too much, what with that, and the hospital, not to mention your family?'

'Believe me, the job keeps me sane,' Catherine assured her. 'And I'd hate to give up the hospital. Some of the children are really in need of someone . . .'

'So are your own children, I guess.'

Stiffly, Catherine said, 'I'm not neglecting my children. Usually I'm home before they are, and they don't feel in the least deprived. They enjoy seeing me on TV.'

'Hold on there!' said Bridie, mildly surprised. 'I wasn't suggesting that you were neglecting them. Just that maybe in doing your duty by them, and the job and the hospital, you could be burdening yourself too much. I know how conscientious you are about your kids. Personally, I think the job is a terrific idea. You've always been a wee bit intense about your family responsibilities, to my mind. It might do you good to have another real interest in life.'

'What do you mean—intense?'

Bridie's face softened. 'Sorry, love. It's none of my business. Forget I said it.'

Catherine was silent for a moment, her eyes puzzled. 'No,' she said finally, 'I'd like to know.'

Bridie bit her lip, and shrugged. 'It's just that sometimes I get the feeling you've wrapped yourself up in Jenny and Michael to such a degree that there's scarcely room for anyone—or anything—else in your life. They grow up awfully fast, you know, and then what will you do? You'll still be a young woman when they leave the nest. Well, anyway, you've proved me wrong. A TV star, no less!'

Catherine smiled. 'Hardly a star. A minor personality is all, honestly. And that only among the youthful population!'

'Great things from little acorns,' said Bridie. 'Etcetera. You're only starting.'

'Then you approve?' Catherine asked almost wistfully.

'Yes, I do. I take it there are some as don't? Jason?'

'Oh, he doesn't object,' said Catherine.

'I see.'

'Why do you say it like that? What do you see?'

'He doesn't object, but he's not wildly enthusiastic, is that it?'

'Something like that,' Catherine admitted. 'Actually, I don't think he takes it at all seriously. It's a whim to keep the little woman happy, as far as he's concerned.'

Bridie looked at her sharply, hearing the waspish note in her voice, and Catherine coloured. 'Well, you know how men are,' she said weakly.

'Sure I do.' Bridie replied instantly, but her eyes were bothered. Changing the subject, she asked, 'Are your in-laws still with you?'

'They go home next week,' Catherine told her, on a note of such relief that Bridie laughed aloud.

'Oh, dear, I know I shouldn't!' Catherine almost wailed. 'They're so awfully good—I haven't had to have a babysitter since they came, and they just shower the children with presents . . .'

'But——' Bridie began with expressive sympathy.

'Oh, you know how it is, having someone else in the house, and I've always felt that Althea didn't quite approve of me, anyway. Even more so, now.'

'Ah! *She's* the one who doesn't approve of you working, I suppose. Am I right?'

'That's certainly part of it. She doesn't say anything directly, but somehow she makes me feel that a real mother would never dream of taking a job if her husband can afford to keep her and the family in any sort of comfort. She's been terribly helpful, actually, and that makes me feel awful about talking of her like this. You won't pass any of this on, though, will you?'

Bridie managed to look mortally offended and funny at the same time, so that Catherine laughed and said quickly, 'I'm sorry! I know you won't. And I'm sorry if I snapped at you before. I think that Althea's attitude has made me over-sensitive to any implied criticism of my working. Even if it wasn't meant at all.'

'Forget it. I guess the strain of having your mother and father-in-law in the house might account for some of that haunted look you've acquired. I'm fantastically lucky with my in-laws. They never interfere, they're always willing to help if we need them, and they're among my closest friends.'

'Sometimes I think the greatest virtue Althea and Winston have is the fact that they live in Australia,' Catherine said wryly. Then immediately she added, 'Oh, that's a terrible thing to say! I don't really mean it.'

'Yeah, I know. They're kind to you.' Bridie nodded exaggeratedly. 'You'd just prefer that they were kind to you from twelve hundred miles away.'

Catherine laughed again. 'Oh, Bridie, you're

good for me! I don't know—I feel so guilty about saying these things.'

'Better to tell someone than bottle it all up till it explodes into a row with your mother-in-law. Let it all hang out, kid. I don't mind being a wailing wall.'

'You're a very good one,' Catherine said gratefully. For a moment it crossed her mind to confide in Bridie the main reason for her strained looks, the ever-increasing estrangement between her and Jason. But even with a friend as understanding as Bridie, she couldn't bring herself to betray such intimate secrets. There wasn't anything anyone else could do about it, and she knew that the obscure sense of guilt she already felt would grow to larger proportions if she did so. If Jason found out, he would never forgive her for discussing their relationship with an outsider.

She went in to the studio one day to find it strangely quiet. Russel was waiting for her, his face grim. 'The technicians have gone on strike,' he told her. 'There won't be any show going out today, unless they just use the segments we've already filmed.'

'I thought they'd sorted out their pay claims,' she said. She had known there was some unrest in the union to which the technical staff belonged, but there had been talks, and she had understood that an agreement was reached and the threat of a strike averted.

'Everyone thought so,' said Russel. 'Then the authorities refused to go along with one clause, and the technicians walked out, after all. Sorry I couldn't let you know before.'

'That's all right. It's not your fault.' She paused, thinking about going back to the house, to Althea and her subtle, sugar-coated criticism. 'Maybe I'll go and do some shopping, or something,' she said vaguely.

'Like to come out to the bach with me instead?' Russel asked unexpectedly.

Catherine's face lit up before she had time to think about it. 'We couldn't,' she said. 'Could we?'

He laughed at her. 'Why not? Let's play hookey for once. It doesn't take that long to get there, and you can phone home and tell them you could be a bit later than usual. Can't you?'

Althea had already promised to watch the children if Catherine was not back when they arrived from school. She hesitated only a moment longer, then said, recklessly, 'Yes. Yes. I could.'

It was rather cooler at the beach now than it had been. The wind off the sea whipped spray back towards the horizon from translucent, frothing breakers, and when they walked along the sand together, small eddies of sand blew stingingly about their ankles. Dark clouds overhung them and eventually smothered the sun, until Russel glanced up and said, 'I think we're in for a downpour any minute. Want to go back?'

Catherine shook her head. The wind and the walking were good. She felt fine, and free for once of the oppressive atmosphere of tension that pervaded her home. The long sweep of clean sand, the thundering of the ocean, somehow made her feel that her problems were insignificant after all, that a little longer in this salt-tangy, invigorating air would clear her mind of its fog of misery and help her to see the way ahead.

The rain came suddenly in the end, huge droplets falling in torrents, so that they were drenched within minutes, scarcely able to see for the downpour. Catherine gasped and laughed, and Russel, his face streaming with water, stripped off his shirt, trying ineffectually to shield her with it, making her laugh again as she thrust it back at him, shaking her head.

He took her hand and they ran stumblingly over the sand, making for the path. He almost hauled her bodily up it, and at the top pushed her ahead of him into the little house.

The slam of the door sounded loud even against the thunder of the rain on the corrugated iron roof. Russel stayed just inside it, shaking himself, while she stood with a smile of amusement on her face, her arms hugging herself against the chill of the water that had saturated her clothes.

Russel saw the smile and grinned back at her. 'We're mad!'

'I'm sorry, I should have agreed to turn back when you suggested it,' she said, but she couldn't help giggling at his bedraggled appearance, his hair plastered down over his forehead, the rain running in little rivers down his bare chest, and one leg of the trousers he had rolled to the knee during their stroll along the beach hanging about a sand-caked ankle.

'You don't look sorry!' He looked pointedly at her own feet, equally sandy, and the hem of her dress spattered with sand and dripping water, and eventually at her face, as she pushed a wet rat's tail of hair away from her mouth. 'And you don't look too soignée yourself.'

She made a face at him. 'I didn't say a word,' she protested innocently.

He snorted disbelievingly. 'You didn't need to. Your face says it all. Don't you know that it's a dead giveaway?'

'You are the one who said I could act!'

'You can. Because you have such an expressive face. It shows all your emotions.'

She made a mock moue at him, and shivered suddenly.

'Hey, you're cold! You'll have to take off those wet things. You can't go home like that!' he told her.

Catherine looked down at herself and suddenly giggled. 'We could say we were interviewing a fish,' she suggested flippantly.

'You're crazy! Get in under the shower and I'll see what I can find for you to wear.'

She did as he said, because obviously it was the most sensible thing. He had given her two beach towels, and when she had rinsed off the sand under the warm stream of water, she wrapped one about her sarong-wise, and turbaned her hair up into the other.

When she emerged, her wrung-out clothes held in her hand, Russel was standing in the middle of the room, holding out a denim shirt. 'It's about the best I can do,' he said. 'I don't keep a ladies' wardrobe here, I'm afraid.'

'I'm glad,' she said simply, eyeing the shirt and mentally trying it for size. 'I think I'll stick to the towel, thanks. It's actually a lot more adequate than that looks.'

'It's big enough,' he agreed. 'Suit yourself. If you're cold, take a blanket from the bed.'

She looked where he indicated, and for the first time really noticed the changes that had taken place since her last visit. When they had arrived, they had simply dropped their shoes on the deck and gone straight down to the beach, and as they ran in from the downpour, she had not taken the time to look about her. Now she saw that the narrow camp bed had been replaced by a wide divan covered with bright striped cotton, and made inviting by several cushions in solid colours to go with the stripes. A thick rich brown sheepskin lay on the varnished floor in front of it, and there was a pile of huge floor cushions in a corner. A cane lounging chair was set where it commanded a view of the sea.

'I've strung a sort of line in the kitchen area that you can hang those wet things on,' said Russel. 'Switch on the fan heater under them, and they should dry.'

She found the line and the heater while he was showering, and directed the fan on the wet clothing. Then she rubbed her hair nearly dry, and when Russel came back, dressed in the denim shirt and matching pants, she asked for a comb, since she had left her bag in the car and hers was in it.

She sat on the lounger, tugging the comb through the tangled mass of her hair, until he came over and said, 'Here, let me try.'

He carefully teased out the snarls with remarkable patience as she sat half turned from him. By the time he had finished her hair was half dry, lying sleekly on her bare shoulders, the ends just beginning to curl.

Russel tossed the comb over on to the end of the bed, and asked, 'Feeling better now?'

'Much, thank you.' Catherine wriggled further back on the lounger and stretched a little.

Russel moved, sitting on the floor, his arm casually resting on the side of the lounger, near her thigh. 'You've been pretty down lately, haven't you?' he said.

'Why do you say that?' she asked cautiously.

'I told you about your face,' he reminded her.

'It doesn't show when I'm working, does it?' She asked, a little on the defensive.

'I told you also that you're a good actress. When you're working you seem happier. It helps you forget, doesn't it?'

It was true, but she said in brittle tones, 'What would I want to forget?'

For a moment Russel was silent. Then he said, 'Don't pretend with me, Cathy. Please.'

Her eyes met his for a heartbeat of time, then she lowered her gaze, saw that her hands were clasped tightly in her lap, over the patterned beach towel. Her voice low, she said, 'I can't talk about it, Russ.'

'Okay.' He waited a moment longer, then got up and went to the window. The rain was still pouring down, the view obscured by the moisture sliding down the glass. 'Just don't try and tell me there's nothing wrong,' he said, with his back to her. 'Because I know that isn't true, and I can't stand to hear you telling gallant little lies.'

It was an odd word to use, and she was strangely touched by it. He thought her gallant. She felt that it was a compliment. When he turned to face her again, she was frowning down at her hands, and he came over and untangled her twisted fingers, and held her hands gently in his as he squatted beside her.

'Relax,' he urged her softly. 'I'm not going to pressure you.'

She withdrew her hands reluctantly from his warm, comforting clasp, and sat up, swinging her feet to the floor. 'Shall I make us some coffee?' she said. 'I think I can remember where everything is.'

She stood up, and Russel followed suit more slowly.

'Help yourself,' he said. His eyes followed her, an unreadable expression in their depths, as she boiled the water and found the coffee, sugar and cups.

'No milk?' she queried.

'There's some tinned cream.' He came into the kitchen area and found it in the cupboard, handing it to her. 'I haven't been out here for a couple of weeks. Supplies are a bit limited. There are some biscuits somewhere, though.'

'Not for me, thanks.' She spooned coffee into the cups and added the boiling water and cream. She sugared hers and pushed the sugar container towards him on the counter, taking her cup over to the table.

'How long do you think the strike will last?' she asked him when he joined her, taking the other chair.

'That's hard to say. Depends on how long the two parties take to reach an agreement, doesn't it?'

Catherine stirred in the sugar and cream and sipped cautiously at the hot brew, her two hands wrapped about the cup. 'You must be fed up. The programme was just beginning to find its feet, wasn't it?'

'You're involved, too. It's pretty depressing for us both.'

'Yes.' She took a gulp of hot liquid that brought tears to her eyes. 'It won't—affect the future of the programme permanently, will it?'

'I shouldn't think so. Don't worry, it'll probably all be over in a day or two, and we'll be back at work.'

'I certainly hope so!'

Russel looked at her strangely. 'You sound as though it's all that stands between you and the wolf at the door.'

'You know it isn't that.'

'But it's important to you, isn't it?'

'I love it,' she said simply. 'I don't know what I'd do if——'

Swiftly, he said, 'You'd find something else. You've got brains and guts, and now that you've struck out on your own you've gained a lot of confidence which was the only thing lacking before. Whatever you decided to do, Cathy, you'd make it.'

She put down her cup to look at him, staring. He looked calm and forceful and his eyes met hers steadily. 'You have a lot of faith in me,' she said strangely.

'Yes. Why don't you have some in yourself? You're terrific, Cathy. I mean that.'

She stood up abruptly and turned her back on him to go over to the window and watch the rain sliding insistently down the panes. Her vision blurred, and she put up a hand to her eyes, biting fiercely on her lower lip.

He came up behind her and tentatively touched her shoulder. 'Cathy?'

She had tried to hold her breath, to contain the tears, but at his touch, the concern in his voice, she was shaken by a heavy, wrenching sob. Russel exclaimed in appalled tones, 'Cathy!' and turned her, his hands on her shoulders, as she sobbed again, unable to stop, the tears running down her face as she tried to hide it from him.

His arms came around her, and after one feebly convulsive effort to free herself, Catherine let him hold her, his cheek against her hair, his hand stroking her shoulder.

After a long time the sobbing became less violent, and she managed to gasp, 'I'm—sorry. I—don't know what——'

'Shh!' he soothed her. 'It's all right, honey.'

He picked her up in his arms, ignoring her murmur of protest, and sat down on the divan, cradling her like a child in his lap. She felt him reach sideways towards the pile of clean clothing on the cupboard nearby, and then a handkerchief, large and unironed but fresh-washed, was pushed into her hand.

The tears kept coming for some time, but at last she leaned against him, exhausted, the dampened handkerchief clasped in her fingers, her hot forehead on his denim-covered shoulder. His hand was soothing her hair, his lips murmuring comfort against her temple.

She gave a long, shuddering sigh, and Russel moved his hand to place his fingers under her chin and raise her face.

'Okay, now?' he asked softly.

'Yes, thank you. I must look awful!'

'You don't look awful. You look beautiful. Vulnerable and hurting, but beautiful.'

He bent his head and she felt the pressure of lips on her burning mouth. His kiss was comforting and sweet and without demand, his lips slightly parted over hers. She sighed again, and her breath went into his mouth. She felt him stiffen, and then the kiss became firmer, his hand sliding to her nape, his other arm folding her gently closer to him.

Catherine knew she should resist, do something about this, but the sensation of warmth and comfort was blissful, and she stayed passive in his arms, too weary to object.

Russel went on kissing her, until the weariness insidiously changed to something else, and the warmth spread through her body. Her mouth quivered under his, and his fingers were spread on her shoulders, and she knew that she had let the moment for resistance pass, that now there was no going back.

She was very late by the time she had collected her car from the studio car-park and driven home. Her heart was thumping as she let herself in the back door, hearing the TV going much too loud in the lounge. She guessed that the children were watching it. The kitchen looked untidy, which surprised her, for Althea's housekeeping was almost fanatical in its neatness. She was about to go through to the lounge when Jason appeared in the doorway. He also looked less immaculate than usual. Although he still wore his business suit, his tie was missing and three buttons on his blue shirt were undone. He was pale, too, and had an angry glitter in his eyes. He stopped in the doorway and demanded explosively, 'Where the *hell* have you *been*? I've been phoning the studio since two o'clock!'

'Two o'clock?' Catherine repeated stupidly. 'Why, whatever's wrong?' Her voice sharpening with panic, she exclaimed, 'The children . . .?'

'The kids are fine,' he told her impatiently. 'It's my father. He's had a heart attack.'

Relief was followed by a sick shock. She placed her bag blindly on the sink counter and put a hand out to him instinctively. 'Oh, Jason! I'm so sorry!'

He ignored the hand, and misunderstood her exclamation of sympathy. 'You damned well ought to be sorry!' he snapped. 'My mother's at the hospital alone, waiting. We don't know yet if Dad's going to pull through. I phoned the studio and they said your car was there, but there was no filming today and they didn't know where you'd gone. One of the neighbours watched for the children coming home, but she had plans for tonight, and when you didn't show up, I had to come home and be with them.'

'Bridie would have——'

'I tried Bridie. I thought you might be there, and if not she would have filled in. I couldn't get hold of her. I thought it wouldn't be long before you came. Where *were* you?'

'At the beach—with a friend.'

'*Beach*?' He cast an incredulous glance at the window behind her. All afternoon there had been intermittent heavy showers, and the wind had become fierce. Then, for the first time, he really looked at her. Her dress was still damp and crushed looking, and sand clung to the hem. Her hair was scarcely dry, and dishevelled again from the wind that had flung around them as Russel and she ran to his car, his arm about her waist. She had hastily put on some lipstick, but her other makeup was gone.

'Beach?' Jason repeated, his eyes suddenly dangerously narrowed. 'What beach? What friend?'

'Karekare,' she whispered. 'Well, near there. With Russel Thurston.'

There was an intense, electric silence. If anything, Jason's face was paler now, and he stared at her with his mouth grim and his eyes a deep, frightening, gunmetal grey.

Catherine felt the hot colour coming up from her throat to stain her face, and stood dumbly, unable to do anything about it. He watched mercilessly. Then he said in a flat voice, 'I see.'

Her throat worked as she tried to say something, anything to take that look off his face, but the words stuck there, refused to come.

At last he moved, coming away from the door. He took two steps into the room, and stood looking down at her, as though he had never seen her before. Finally he said, 'I want to go to the hospital. Do you think that you could manage to look after your own children, now?'

She didn't remind him that they were his children, too. She nodded, and gazed fixedly at the floor as he went out without even stopping to fetch his tie.

When she went into the lounge, the children hardly noticed her. The programme was a crime series that she normally didn't allow them to watch, but tonight she let them see it through to the bloody finale before she sent them to bed.

It was after ten before Jason and Althea returned from the hospital. Althea looked gaunt and old, her pale lips taut and her eyes dull. Jason's face was set in harsh lines as he shepherded his mother into a chair, and Catherine asked, anxiously, 'How is he?'

'Sleeping peacefully,' Jason said curtly, not looking at her. 'They say he'll probably pull through this time, but of course he'll be in hospital for a while.'

'Oh, thank God!' Catherine breathed, and Althea looked up at her, then turned her head against the back of the chair and closed her eyes.

Catherine asked, 'Would you like some tea, Althea—or cocoa, something hot?'

'Or a sherry,' said Jason. 'What'll it be, Mother?'

Althea just shook her head fretfully, and for the first time in her life Catherine was wrung with pity for the older woman.

She went over to the chair, noticing with one corner of her mind that Jason moved abruptly away as she approached, and knelt in front of Althea, touching her arm. 'You should have something, you know,' she said gently. 'Will you let Jason pour you a small sherry, or shall I make you a hot drink? Have you had anything to eat?'

Jason said, 'We had some sandwiches and coffee hours ago.'

Althea said faintly, 'I don't want anything.'

'I'll make you some soup,' Catherine decided, and got up. 'And then I'll help you to bed.'

'I don't need help!' Althea said quite sharply. 'I'm not the one who's sick.'

She suddenly put her head down on her hand and began to weep noisily, while Catherine and Jason stood in astonished silence. Then Jason moved swiftly to kneel by his mother and put his arm about her, while she turned blindly to rest her head against his shoulder.

Catherine stood transfixed, watching the tenderness of Jason's handling of his mother, and thinking confusedly of how she herself had turned for comfort to another man. Then Jason half-turned and, without looking at her face, said brusquely, 'Get that soup, will you?'

By the time she had opened a packet of dried soup and heated it, and brought it in on a tray with fingers of toast, Althea was sitting calmly in the chair, only slightly red-eyed, and Jason was prowling about the room with his hands in his pockets.

Catherine had been afraid that Althea would turn down the snack after all, but she merely said, 'Thank you, dear,' and almost finished the bowl, although she didn't touch the toast.

'Do you want some, Jason?' Catherine asked. 'There's more in the pot. I'll get it——'

'No!' The negative stopped her as she made a tentative move to return to the kitchen.

For a moment their eyes met, and she read a cold contempt in his, and flinched from it. She went to stand by Althea's chair, taking the bowl from her as she put the spoon down.

'Don't you want the toast?' she asked evenly.

Althea shook her head.

'More soup?'

'No, thank you, Catherine. That was very nice. I think I'll go to bed now. Please—I don't need any help.'

She got up slowly, and Catherine thought of her mother-in-law's usual brisk, decisive movements, and felt her heart contract with pity. 'I'm sorry I wasn't here when it happened,' she said. 'It must have been awful.'

Althea's mouth quivered, then straightened thinly. 'Yes,' she said. 'After I'd phoned the ambulance, I rang Jason, of course. He was trying to contact you all afternoon, but they said you were not at the studio.'

'I'm sorry,' Catherine repeated. 'There's a technicians' strike on, and we couldn't do any taping, so I—went out for the afternoon. It was terribly bad luck that this had to happen today.'

Althea nodded tiredly and said, 'Yes—well, never mind. Let's hope that they're right, and he will recover.'

Jason went over and held the door for her, even though it was already open. He watched her go down the passage to the spare room, while Catherine stood with the tray in her hands, unwilling to pass him while he remained there.

But after a few moments he closed the door and stood in front of it, leaning his shoulder against the wood, his arms folded.

'Terribly bad luck, wasn't it?' he said with soft sarcasm. 'It was very inconsiderate of my father to have a heart attack just when you were having a session with your lover.'

She winced. 'Jason,' she said huskily, 'I don't

think either of us is in a fit state to discuss this just now. You must have had a dreadful day——'

'I'm glad you realise that!' he cut in savagely. 'It's been, to put it mildly, a hell of a day. I thought my father was going to die, and my mother was going out of her mind with fear and with worrying about not being here when Jenny and Michael came home, and I couldn't find you! I must admit the one thing that didn't occur to me was that you were busy being unfaithful to me. How long have you been sleeping with him? Or isn't that the right word? You actually do sleep with *me*, don't you? And that is literally all! I should have guessed at the reason. It was pretty stupid of me not to. Is he the first? Or the only one? How many others have there been—are there?'

'*Jason!*'

'It's a logical question, my darling wife. You see, it never even crossed my mind before to doubt your fidelity. Now I can't help wondering just how much of a fool I've been.'

'You haven't been a fool at all. I'm not—like that!'

'Aren't you? I saw your face when you came in today—guilt personified. You even *smelled* of him!'

Horrified, Catherine knew she was blushing again, the telltale heat flooding her cheeks. 'Jason, please!' she pleaded weakly, her voice trembling. 'Don't talk like this. I haven't been—we're not——'

'Are you telling me you haven't slept with Russel Thurston?' he demanded harshly.

'I'm telling you——' she managed, '—— that it's never happened before.'

His mouth curled with contempt. 'You mean you've never been found out before!'

'*No*, Jason! I swear——'

'Where?' he interrupted in a hard voice. 'I'm curious to know where you were all the time I was trying to find you this afternoon. In some sleazy little motel room? Or does he take you home? He isn't married, is he?'

'Does it matter?' She heard the bowl rattle against the tray in her hands, and carefully put the tray down on a side table. When she straightened, she found that he had moved away from the door and was standing close to her, his eyes blazing. She started in surprised fear, and Jason wrapped his fingers about her arm in a painful grip, and demanded, 'Where were you?'

'At the beach,' she said. 'I told you. He—he has a bach there.'

His fingers tightened until she gasped. His voice low and steely, he said, 'You've been there before. Haven't you?'

'Yes,' she admitted. 'But——'

He released her arm and turned away from her, his whole attitude one of disgust. 'At every opportunity, no doubt. Is it a nice little love-nest?'

'It isn't a love-nest. As a matter of fact, it's rather primitive——'

'But very private!'

'Jason, this has nothing to do with——'

'I think it has a great deal to do with the subject under discussion. I'm curious.'

Catherine looked at his face, shocked, and saw that he was wearing an expression of extreme cynicism. His eyes glittered coldly, and his mouth had a sardonic twist.

With a sudden spurt of temper, she said, 'What's the next question, then? Do you want to know what sort of lover he is?'

For a moment she thought Jason was going to

hit her. But he controlled his evident rage immediately, and said smoothly, 'Yes, enlighten me. I take it he's better than I am.'

She turned away, sickened, but he caught her arm and twisted her to face him. 'Go on,' he gritted. *'Tell me!'*

She tried to pull away from him, but he stilled her struggles with both hands, hurting her, and she felt a renewal of her own hot anger, and flung back her head to look at him defiantly, saying, 'All right! He's better! He's very gentle and understanding, and that's more than can be said for you!'

Jason's mouth compressed in an ugly line, and his voice was clipped. 'Thank you,' he said.

He had asked for it, goaded her into saying it, but her fury died in sick despair and disgust, and she whispered, 'I'm sorry, Jason, I didn't mean to say it. I'm sorry about—everything.'

'Sorry is scarcely adequate,' he said coldly. He let her go suddenly, as though he couldn't bear to go on touching her, and with a strangely clumsy movement he scooped up the tray from the table, walking towards the door. 'You'd better go to bed,' he said. 'I won't be joining you tonight.'

'What will you do?' she asked foolishly.

In the doorway he paused, and looked at her. 'I'll sleep here.' As he saw her face change, he added, 'I'll be up before my mother wakes. I don't suppose I'll sleep much anyway.'

Catherine heard him washing up, and went slowly to the bathroom and then to bed. She hadn't expected to sleep much, either, but after waiting for an hour, she realised that Jason wasn't even going to fetch his pyjamas from their room, and soon afterwards she fell into a deep, totally exhausted sleep.

CHAPTER EIGHT

WHEN Jason telephoned the hospital the following morning, he was told his father was comfortable after a good night. The news lessened slightly the strain on Althea's face, and Catherine breathed a quiet prayer of thanks.

Jason drove his mother to the hospital straight after breakfast, and Catherine took the children to school. They were subdued, and Jenny looked apprehensive, her green eyes anxious.

'Grandpa is feeling much better this morning,' Catherine assured them. 'Pretty soon I expect they'll let him come home.'

Jenny looked relieved, and Michael wanted to know why they couldn't go and visit him in the hospital.

'He needs to rest very quietly for a while,' Catherine explained. 'But if he's going to be there a few more days, you may be allowed to see him.'

'In school time?' Michael enquired hopefully, and Catherine gave a shaky laugh and said,

'Probably not. Hospitals have evening visiting hours, too, you know.'

After she returned to the house, she washed up the breakfast dishes and then wandered aimlessly through the rooms, picking up toys and books and putting them down in a different place, straightening cushions, then standing staring into space for minutes at a time.

Eventually she mentally shook herself, and forced her hands to carry out routine tasks, bedmaking, sorting clothes into the washing machine, vacuuming the carpet.

It was nearly lunchtime when she thought with a sudden jolt that she ought to phone the studio and find out what was happening. She stood looking at the telephone, reluctant to lift the handset, wondering what she would say if they put her on to Russel.

She jumped when the bell suddenly shrilled at her, and she let it ring three times before nerving herself to pick up the receiver.

It was Russel. 'We're back in business,' he told her, so casually that she was sure he was not alone. 'The usual time tomorrow.'

'Russel?' she said urgently.

'Yes?' His voice was guarded, he was afraid she was going to say something intimate, and he didn't want other people to hear.

'My father-in-law had a heart attack,' she told him. 'Yesterday.'

There was a brief, telling silence. 'My God!' he muttered softly. Again there was silence, and she could almost hear him marshalling his thoughts, assessing the implications. Then he said, 'I'm sorry, Cathy, really sorry. How is he?'

'Better this morning, apparently,' she said, her voice slightly hoarse with effort. 'He'll be in hospital for a while, of course.'

'Of course. Can you make it, tomorrow?'

'I think so. I'll let you know if I'm not able to get there.'

'Okay.' Again he paused. 'Is there anything I can do?'

'Nothing, thank you.'

'Well, you know you only have to say . . .'

'Yes. Thank you. Goodbye.' Catherine put the receiver down clumsily, and stood holding it with

her fingers tight and slippery on the cream plastic.
She took a deep, shuddering breath and, releasing
her grip slowly, went into the kitchen, opened the
fridge and stared blankly at its contents for several
minutes. She shut the door again and leaned her
forehead against the cool enamelled surface,
closing her eyes.

She jumped when the door opened, and Jason's
voice said sharply, 'What's the matter? Are you all
right?'

He had come in with his mother, they were both
standing just inside the door, staring at her.

Hastily she straightened away from the refrigerator. 'I didn't hear the car,' she said. 'I'm all
right, thank you. Just a bit tired. How is Winston?'

'They say they expect he'll be fine in a couple of
weeks. He'll have to be a bit careful, though, from
now on. Just as well he's retired.'

Catherine looked at Althea and saw that she
was looking more herself, cool and in command,
though the hollow shadows under her eyes hadn't
shifted, and there were deep lines showing by her
mouth. 'That's good,' she said. 'I'll make some
lunch. Why don't you go and put your feet up in
the lounge for a while, Althea?'

'No, I'd rather help,' said Althea. 'I need to do
something . . .'

Catherine didn't want her help, but she saw that
Althea was still unable to quite believe in the
hopeful verdict. 'Perhaps you might set the table
for us, then,' she said. 'Is cold meat and salad all
right?'

'Yes, of course.'

'I'm not staying,' said Jason. 'I must get to the
office. There'll be a backlog waiting, and getting
worse all the time. I've already had my secretary
cancel three appointments.'

Catherine tried not to show her relief. She was turning to open the fridge again when he said, 'If my mother wants to visit Dad again this afternoon, could you take her?'

'Yes, of course.'

'I may be late tonight,' he told her. 'But I'll be back in time to take Mother for evening visiting.'

'Would the children be allowed to see him?' she asked. 'They're very anxious.'

'Not yet. Maybe later.' He paused with his hand on the door knob. 'I hope you'll be able to keep Mother company over the next few days, when I can't be here.'

Dismayed, she said, 'But the strike is over. I have to work tomorrow—and regularly after that.'

Jason's mouth compressed. 'Can't they get someone to stand in for you? It's only a children's programme, after all.'

'Some people think children are important,' she said huskily, more hurt than he could know by the dismissal in his voice.

He made an impatient gesture. 'I don't mean that! There's a crisis on here, for God's sake!'

Unexpectedly, his mother intervened. Briskly, she said, 'Nonsense, Jason. The crisis was yesterday. There's no need for Catherine to hold my hand all day. I shall be perfectly all right. Perhaps she could drop me off at the hospital when she goes in to work.'

'Of course I will,' Catherine said quickly, once she had recovered from her surprise. 'And I'll see if Bridie can have the children after school.'

'There's no need,' said Althea. 'I can get a taxi home and be here when they arrive.'

'Oh, please don't——' Catherine started.

'No, I insist!' her mother-in-law said. 'I have to keep busy. I'm sure it's best.'

'Well—all right,' Catherine agreed rather reluctantly.

Jason said nothing, but she thought he was displeased. 'I'll put Bridie on standby, anyway,' she promised. 'And the high school girl who babysits for us sometimes. Then if for any reason you can't make it, just phone the studio and I'll arrange for one of them to take over.'

Jason opened the door and went out without another word, closing it with a snap behind him.

The two women ate in virtual silence. Althea picked at her food without interest, and drank two cups of tea, and Catherine, too, found it difficult to force herself to eat.

They had just washed up the dishes when someone rang the bell at the front door.

Catherine went to answer it, and found Russel standing on the little porch.

'Hello, Cathy,' he said quietly, as she stared at him in faint shock. 'Can I come in?'

Althea had come into the passageway from the kitchen, and was standing watching them. Catherine stepped back, and Russel walked into the carpeted hall. He looked past her at Althea, and Catherine turned and said, 'Althea, this is my boss, Russel Thurston. Russel, this is my mother-in-law, Mrs Clyde.'

Althea held out a cool hand. 'How do you do, Mr Thurston. We've heard a lot about you.'

He shook her hand and said, 'I've heard something of you too, Mrs Clyde, and of your husband's illness. I'm sorry about it. I wondered if there was any way I could help.'

'That's very kind of you, Mr Thurston. Catherine, aren't you going to ask your visitor into the lounge?'

'Yes, of course,' said Catherine. She gestured to the doorway, and led the way. Althea came, too, seating herself in one of the armchairs.

Russel cast Catherine an unreadable look as he waited for her to sit down before taking a chair himself. 'I won't stay long,' he said. 'If you're not in need of anything . . .'

'Thank you, Russel, we're coping quite well,' Catherine told him. 'He's apparently quite a lot better. They expect him to recover.'

'That's good.' He looked at her again, and she saw that there was a message in his eyes that he was trying to hide from Althea.

She became a little panicky, because Althea was very astute. She dragged her eyes from his and said, 'Would you like a cup of tea or coffee, Russel?'

'No, I've just come from lunch, thanks.' There was an awkward pause, which Althea seemingly felt must be filled. In her most social manner, she leaned forward a little and said, 'You have a most interesting job, Mr Thurston, don't you? I'm sure you must have met so many fascinating people.'

He turned to her almost with relief, smiling as he agreed. She kept him on the subject for some time, and Catherine sat almost totally silent, tense in her chair.

When he rose to go, she went with him to the door, while Althea remained in the lounge.

At the door he grasped Catherine's arm lightly and took her outside with him. In a low voice, he said, 'Cathy, I'm sorry—your husband was trying to contact you all yesterday afternoon, and the staff could see your car in the car-park, they knew we'd left together——'

She looked up at him with a pale face and shadowed eyes, and he made an exclamation under his breath and said, 'I wish I could take you in my arms here and now——'

Instinctively she made a small movement away from him, and he smiled grimly and said, 'Don't. I won't touch you—not right now. I just thought you should be warned. I don't think that anyone will say much to you—though I've taken a bit of flak already. Still, they can't really know anything, except the fact that we were together.'

'I see,' she said woodenly.

'Cathy,' he breathed, pain in his eyes. 'I hadn't planned it, you know. But I can't pretend to be sorry for what happened. I'm only sorry that it's maybe caused some gossip that could embarrass you. I suppose if your husband hears it——'

'Jason knows.'

After a moment's silence, he said, 'Did you tell him?'

'He—guessed.'

Russel groaned, raising his eyes. 'Oh, honey, your face! I told you about it, didn't I?'

'I think—I would have told him, anyway,' she admitted.

'Yes,' he agreed soberly, 'I guess you would. You're too honest to hide a thing like that.' He bit his lip briefly and asked, 'How did he take it?'

'How would you expect him to take it?' she asked him.

His mouth compressed. 'Yes, I see. Where do we go from here, Cathy?'

She looked at him steadily, something inside her contracting in misery. 'Nowhere,' she said calmly.

His eyes searched hers. 'If that's how you want it,' he said slowly. 'It's over, just like that, is it?'

'That's right.' Her voice was barely a whisper.

'That easily?'

She quivered at the slight, bitter note of accusation in his voice, and momentarily closed her eyes. 'I didn't say it was easy, Russ. It isn't going to be easy.'

'I—suppose——' he said, 'I took advantage of you, didn't I? Caught you in a weak moment——?'

'No, Russ, you took no advantage. Don't think that I blame you—please. You know——' she flushed slightly, '—— the feeling was mutual.'

His eyes gleamed. 'Thanks for that, anyway. You won't leave the programme, will you? I promise not to make things hard for you.'

A smile glimmered. 'Do all men manage to put their work first?'

'I wasn't.' He spoke quietly, but with force. 'I was thinking of you. You love it, you know you do. I don't want you to feel you have to sacrifice it to your conscience—or your husband.'

A strange melting warmth seemed to trickle through her. That constant, genuine concern for her was still there, and it had always been very seductive. 'Thank you, Russ,' she said, her eyes stinging with tears. 'You're so—no wonder I——'

She turned away and went blindly back to the house, pausing inside the door after she had carefully closed it, to take several deep breaths and control the threat of tears. She heard the car drive away, and Althea came out of the lounge and said, 'I think I will lie down for half an hour, Catherine, after all. Then perhaps we could go back to the hospital. Will that give you time to be home before the children?'

It would, Catherine said, amazed that the other woman noticed nothing wrong. She felt wrung out, haggard. But then, Althea probably felt even more so. She was in no state to take particular notice of other people's emotional crises.

Althea told Jason that evening, when he was seated in the lounge drinking coffee after a late dinner, that Russel had called. 'A very pleasant young man,' she said tranquilly. 'It was kind of him to take the trouble to come round and offer sympathy and help, don't you think?'

Catherine saw the cup in Jason's hand still in mid-air before he raised it to his mouth. 'Very kind,' he said unemotionally, as he replaced the cup in its saucer. His eyes found hers, a deep blaze of contempt in them. 'He's done a great deal for Catherine already, of course.'

Catherine knew she had gone cold, trying not to flinch from that gaze. Althea said calmly, 'Yes, I know that he was the one who persuaded her to go on the TV show. And I don't think he's regretted it.'

'I'm sure he hasn't,' Jason said smoothly, his eyes still holding Catherine's.

'He said she's very good, though at first she was lacking in confidence, a little. However, I daresay that was better than over-confidence. He said it's been very easy to teach her the right techniques.'

'I'll bet,' Jason murmured, but Althea seemed not to notice the fleetingly ugly expression on his handsome face. Catherine, suppressing a shudder, turned away, wrenching her eyes at last from his cruel stare.

She went to bed early, hoping that he would stay in the lounge talking to his mother until she could reasonably pretend to be sleeping. But he came soon afterwards, as she was standing in her nightdress before the mirror, taking pins from her hair.

She picked up the pretty silver-backed brush with the flowered design that he had given her for her birthday two years ago, and nervously began using it.

When he came near, she felt her skin shiver, and it was all she could do not to jump when he leaned close, but he only placed his keys and some small change on the dressing table, then walked over to the big wardrobe as he shrugged out of his jacket.

She wondered where he was going to sleep, but didn't dare to ask. She put down the brush, knowing that he had removed his shirt and was unbuckling his belt. She stood fiddling with the things on the dressing table, moving the hand mirror over a few inches, picking up a cut crystal scent bottle and putting it down again.

Jason had pulled on maroon pyjama trousers before he spoke, saying harshly, 'So lover-boy couldn't keep away from you today? Was he very put out when he found my mother here to chaperone you?'

'It wasn't like that,' Catherine protested.

'No? He came just to offer his condolences and see if he could help, did he?'

'Yes,' she said, knowing that she sounded unconvincing. He hadn't come just for that, of course. He had hoped to see her alone, to warn her about the gossip that might be circulating. She didn't want to tell Jason that. It was bad enough that he knew himself, without being made aware that the whole of the television studio staff were making only too accurate surmises.

'You're a bad liar,' he said, coming over to her. She turned to face him fully, trying not to show how nervous he made her.

He took her chin in a hard hold and his eyes glittered into hers. 'I don't want him in my house,' he grated. 'Ever again, understand? Don't you *ever* invite him here again!'

'I didn't invite him,' she protested.

'No, I don't suppose you did,' he said cynically. 'Not knowing my mother was here. He's a bit too eager, isn't he?'

'Jason, please stop it. I know you're angry, but——'

'Angry? You have a genius for understatement, darling. I'll tell you something. I always thought of myself as a civilised human being, but in the last two days I've realised just how primitive emotions can be. I would take the greatest pleasure in beating your boy-friend to a bloody pulp—and what I'd like to do to you doesn't bear thinking about. Like breaking every bone in your body, for starters. Does that frighten you? It should. It terrifies me. So don't—*don't* give me any excuses, Catherine.'

Her eyes wide, she shivered in his hold. She had always known that Jason had a capacity for violence that he kept under rigid control. Now it threatened to escape that control, he had admitted it. She was mute, afraid to speak.

He released her abruptly and muttered, 'I'm going to the bathroom.'

Catherine got into bed, still shivering in spite of the blankets. She closed her eyes, and fifteen minutes later he came back and slid into bed beside her, not touching her, but only inches away. She lay tense, trying to keep her breathing even, every muscle rigid.

When he moved, her hands clenched by her sides and her eyes flew wide in the darkness. His hand was on her waist, and when it slid up to her breast and rested there, she held her breath. Jason shifted his body, his hard thigh coming between hers, and his hand stroked up to her shoulder until his fingers were on her neck, the thumb lightly pressing on her throat as he lowered his mouth and kissed her.

She had almost expected naked savagery, her mouth quivering under his with apprehension. But although it was hard and brooked no refusal, his kiss was not cruel. She raised a tentative hand to his shoulder, and he lifted his mouth abruptly and with his fingers on her wrist forced her hand back down on the pillow. 'Jason,' she whispered.

He said, 'Be quiet. Just be quiet,' and kissed her again, parting her lips forcibly, moving his mouth back and forth over hers.

His hands on her body caressed her with controlled violence, and he stilled every move she tried to make, just stopping short of hurting her. Her heart was thumping with fear and something else, and she accepted the message of his body and lay quietly as he made love to her in a totally new, totally puzzling way. He wanted her only to be passive, not to stir at all, either in resistance or in reciprocation. In the end she felt that he had reduced her to some sort of object, a thing for his own use, reasserting his ownership as though she was a possession that had been illegally borrowed by someone else.

It was the first time he had ever had a total lack of care for her feelings during lovemaking, and when it was over she had tears slipping silently down her cheeks.

Jason felt them on his fingers as he released her, sliding his hands away from her face where he had been holding her while his mouth kept hers captive.

He lay on his back, breathing hard, then said, 'If it makes any difference, I didn't enjoy that much, either.'

Catherine wiped away the tears with the sheet, and swallowed. Her eyes were burning and sore, and she shut them, tightly.

'Go to sleep,' Jason said harshly.

She swallowed again, biting fiercely on her lower lip. She felt humiliated and wildly unhappy, and she wanted to die. To go to sleep and never, never wake up.

CHAPTER NINE

CATHERINE had to nerve herself to turn up at the studio the next day, but although she thought there were a few covertly interested looks cast at her and Russel, nothing was said. Russel helped, his manner so normal and unchanged that she was soon able to take her cue from him and appear quite unconcerned and unaware.

Winston recovered gradually in the next two weeks, but of course his and Althea's return trip had been postponed. Catherine resigned herself to having them both stay for at least another two weeks after Winston had been discharged from the hospital. She felt guilty because the prospect filled her with dread, but at the same time there was a measure of relief in the thought that not yet would she be alone with Jason, apart from the children. There had been no repeat of the coldblooded lovemaking which had shocked and distressed her, and in front of his mother she and Jason managed somehow to maintain a façade of normality. But in the privacy of their own room, an icy estrangement prevailed between them, the tension at snapping point every evening.

The children seemed not to have noticed the strain. There were times, when the whole family was together, when both Catherine and Jason tried so hard to pretend there was nothing wrong, that she could almost believe it herself. Then he would catch her eye, and she would see the bleak enmity in his, and hastily look away.

Several times she tried to make an opportunity

to talk to him, to try and get through the invisible barrier that seemed to divide them from each other as effectively as a brick wall. Each time she retreated in failure, defeated by his apparent indifference or his occasional biting sarcasm.

One evening there was an office party which Jason was expected to attend, and to bring his wife to. Catherine would have seized on any excuse not to accompany him, but Althea had offered to babysit, and when she dared to suggest that she would prefer to stay home, Jason turned on her with a savage expression and said, 'You'll come, Catherine, if I have to drag you by the hair. I know you'd rather be anywhere else but with me, but you can at least pretend to act like a wife!'

So she went to the party, suitably dressed in a long, dark synthetic dress that left her shoulders bare and skimmed her slim figure seductively, and with her hair newly shampooed and styled in pretty tendrils about her face.

The occasion was a farewell for a long-serving member of the senior staff, with cocktails served for over a hundred people, and dinner afterwards for the 'inner circle' of senior staff. She found herself singled out by many as someone other, now, than simply Jason's wife. Several people made a point of mentioning her TV performances, and asking her questions about how the show was made. She found that although at first she felt rather selfconscious, it was far more pleasant being able to talk about the work which she found fascinating than, as on previous occasions, searching for small talk with the wives, and listening to Jason's colleagues as they 'talked shop.' By the time dinner was served, she had begun to almost enjoy herself, and she even had

enough confidence, after a couple of glasses of
sherry, to boldly ask one of the men what was
meant by a term he used when speaking to Jason
of some aspect of business leases.

Jason looked surprised, but the other man
smiled and apologised, saying, 'I'm sorry, Mrs
Clyde, we shouldn't be boring you with this stuff.'

'It's only boring because I don't understand it,'
she answered. 'Could you explain to me what "nil
residual" means? I'm interested.'

He did, and she asked more questions, and got a
short and simple lesson on some aspects of high
finance. Jason stood by watching them both, with
his half full glass in his hand, and when the man
had excused himself and gone to speak to another
couple, he asked quietly, his eyes fixed on her with
a frown, 'What was that all about?'

'It was about lease contracts,' she said lightly.
'Weren't you listening?'

'I could have told you everything you ever
wanted to know about lease contracts,' he
reminded her. 'You've never wanted to know.'

'Well, now I do. Going to work has broadened
my horizons——'

'Don't I know it!' he muttered under his breath.
'What are you up to now? Looking for new fields
to conquer? I should warn you, Harding is a very
happily married man, with five children, no less.
And a good, churchgoing Catholic. You're not
likely to get far with him.'

She regarded him steadily. He had baited her
like this before, and usually she found it so
shattering that she could do nothing but turn
away, sick with guilt and hurt, and only
determined to hide her tears from him. Perhaps the
sherry she had drunk helped, but suddenly she
realised that if she went on accepting everything

Jason threw at her, the blame, the studied insults, the vicious innuendoes, her life was not going to be worth living. This couldn't go on without it becoming a pernicious habit, a sort of sado-masochistic ritual.

The time had come to break the pattern. 'That was uncalled for,' she said. 'You know perfectly well that I wasn't even mildly flirting with the man. It was a conversation that he might have had with anyone who didn't move in the same business circles.'

She saw the surprise in his eyes, quickly succeeded by calculation as though he was sizing up an opponent. 'All right,' he said at last, 'I withdraw that remark.'

'Thank you,' Catherine said coolly, and held out her glass. 'May I have another sherry?'

Jason cast her a sharp look, and went to the bar. When he came back she was talking to one of the women executives, and they were exchanging views on the problems and challenges of raising a family while engaged in a career.

'It certainly helps if you have a co-operative husband,' the other woman was saying as Jason joined them. 'Jason, have you been doing more dishes since your wife went to work?' she asked him teasingly.

'Jason's mother and father have been with us since just after I got the job,' Catherine said quickly. 'Althea looks after the children quite often.'

'You're lucky,' the woman said. 'I have to hire a babysitter when I'm working past school time.'

'I will, too, once Jason's parents leave,' said Catherine.

Jason looked at her sharply, then lowered his eyes as he sipped at his drink.

They went in to dinner soon afterwards, and were served several courses, beginning with tua tua soup and ending with the traditional pavlova topped with whipped cream and red tamarillo slices dusted with sugar. Catherine drank three glasses of white wine made from locally grown grapes at Henderson, Auckland's nearby wine district, and by the end of the meal felt pleasantly stimulated. She had scarcely spoken to Jason, but carried on an animated conversation with her neighbour on the other side, who was in the marketing side of the financial firm. They were deep in a lively debate on the value and uses of television advertising when the chairman rose at the head of the table and called for order.

'Speeches!' Catherine's neighbour groaned. 'Old Shorter can go on for hours.'

Mr Shorter did discourse at some length about the years that Arthur Baysting, the guest of honour, had spent in the firm, and how he had worked up to his present top management position after starting work as an office boy way back in the Dark Ages. But Catherine's table companion kept her amused with irreverent whispered asides and additional remarks, so that she was obliged to choke back laughter, pressing her napkin to her mouth to hide her amusement.

After the Chairman, Mr Baysting's department head made a briefer, wittier speech, and one of his colleagues who had worked with him for forty years insisted on saying a few more words of praise, studded with anecdotes.

A flurry of wine-pouring went on round the table as the Chairman rose again, to propose a toast to Arthur and wish him all the best in his retirement, adding that Arthur might have made fifty years in harness, if a slightly earlier retirement had not been forced upon him by his doctor's recommendation after his recent illness. Then, with a final injunction to Arthur not to over-exert himself, and to enjoy a long and peaceful retirement, the Chairman cast an expert eye about the table, noted that everyone had a full glass, and proposed the toast they had been waiting for.

Everyone rose, and Jason leaned forward and pulled back Catherine's chair, his cheek brushing against her temple as he straightened. She jerked her face aside, upsetting her balance, and he grabbed at her arm to steady her. His grip was like steel, and it didn't relax until they had drunk the toast and were seated again.

The toast had included Arthur's wife, a thin, nervous-looking woman who sat beside him in blue brocade and a brown fur stole, smiling shyly as he rose, pink-faced and embarrassed, to reply to the toast.

He spoke at first hesitantly, and then with growing confidence, lacing his speech with well-rehearsed in-jokes which amused his colleagues but often left the other guests slightly puzzled. He reviewed his rise through the firm, with painful slowness, until Catherine felt slightly glassy-eyed, wondering when the catalogue of achievements and funny incidents would reach its end. Then he seemed about to wind down, but first he had a list of people who apparently deserved his thanks, starting with his wife, and progressing through the Chairman and several of his predecessors. Catherine had virtually stopped listening, clamping her jaws to stop a yawn escaping, and fixing a determinedly interested expression on her face, when she heard Jason's name mentioned.

'. . . . and most certainly not least,' Arthur was

saying ponderously, 'my young friend Jason
Clyde, who probably saved my life.'

He was looking down the table, smiling at
Jason, who made a dismissive gesture with his
hand and frowned, muttering, 'Nonsense!'

But Arthur would not be stopped. 'That's a day
I'll never forget,' he said. 'I never knew before what a
heart attack was like. Well, now I do know, and I
don't want to experience it again, thank you.'

Several cries and murmurs of encouragement
came from the men about the table, but Arthur
spoke over them. 'I want to publicly thank you,
Jason,' he said solemnly. 'You brought me round
and sent for the ambulance, and if you hadn't
acted so promptly, I might not be standing here
tonight.'

A ripple of applause followed, and Arthur
beamed at Jason, who had lowered his head to
stare fixedly at the white tablecloth, his mouth
turned down. It was the first time that Catherine
had ever seen Jason looking acutely embarrassed.
And Arthur had not finished yet. 'And then,' he
went on, beaming about at the other guests, 'he
went himself to see my wife and take her to the
hospital, where he stayed with her until my son
arrived from Hamilton several hours later. Thank
you, not just for me, but on behalf of my family,
Jason. We want you to know that we appreciate
your actions.'

Jason, tightlipped, gave a jerky nod as more
applause followed, and Arthur added a few more
words of general thanks and appreciation for the
function honouring his retirement.

Later the guests rose from the table and, as
informal groups gathered preparatory to depar-
ture, Jason took Catherine's arm to say goodbye
to Arthur and his wife.

Arthur took Jason's hand in both of his, smiling widely, obviously pleased with himself.

'Goodbye, Arthur,' said Jason. 'Look after yourself. If I'd known you were going to do what you did in that speech tonight, I'd have left you there on the floor when it happened!'

Arthur laughed. 'I meant every word!' he said. 'Mrs Clyde, your husband's a man to be very proud of.'

'He was so kind,' Mrs Baysting said softly, hanging on to her husband's arm. 'He broke the news so gently to me, and insisted on taking me to the hospital himself. He stayed even after they said Arthur was going to be all right.'

'I'm glad he was able to help,' said Catherine. 'Goodnight, and very best wishes for a long and pleasant retirement for both of you.'

'Oh, I'm not retiring,' Mrs Baysting said with shy playfulness. 'Women never do, do they? In fact, I expect I'll be busier than ever with Arthur home all day. I'm not used to having him there for lunch—and then he's accustomed to having his morning and afternoon teas, you know. I seldom bother, on my own. I daresay we'll both get fat!'

She seemed happy enough at the prospect, Catherine reflected as they moved away to make room for other guests to bid their farewells.

'You never told me you'd saved a man's life,' she said to Jason as they waited for the lift to take them down to the ground floor and the car-park.

Jason shrugged. 'He's blown it up out of proportion. All I did was what anyone with a bit of common sense would have done.'

'What? Mouth-to-mouth? Heart massage?'

'A bit of both. I've never done it in earnest before. I was very relieved to see the ambulance blokes come in, I can tell you.'

'You must have done some good while you were waiting.'

'So they said.'

The lift arrived, the doors opening for them as another couple came from the dining room and hurried to join them while Jason held the door button.

She was silent in the lift, only saying, when the other couple had called their goodnights and Jason was unlocking the car door, 'How long ago did it happen?'

'What?'

'This heart attack of Arthur's.'

He seemed to hesitate before he opened the door for her and said, 'Does it matter?'

His voice was indifferent, and she said, 'I suppose not.' It must have been recently, she guessed—since they had virtually stopped speaking to each other. It was a frightening thought, that they had grown so far apart that she had known nothing about so dramatic an experience, which must have involved him so closely. And since his own father's attack, he must have found the memories of it jarring. Yet he had said nothing about it to her.

It wasn't until he had slid into his own seat and fastened his safety belt that he said, 'Actually, it was some months back. The day we were supposed to have had lunch together, remember?'

CHAPTER TEN

CATHERINE was stunned. 'Why didn't you *tell* me?' she asked him

Jason was turning the key, bringing the engine to life, and he had backed out of the parking space and driven the car out of the car-park gateway before he replied.

'I tried to tell you,' he said. 'You didn't want to know.'

She was silenced. She remembered now that he had wanted to explain to her why he had cancelled their lunch, and she had stopped him, preferring not to hear what particular business crisis was more important than his wife.

She started to say something, her hands clenching in her lap, then her voice died as she saw the remote set of his profile in the light from a street lamp. What could she say? 'I'm sorry,' was such an inadequate phrase in this instance. And she was very sure that Jason didn't want to hear it.

Back home, they found the house in darkness except for the porch light that Althea had left on for them. Catherine peeped into the children's rooms, saw them sound asleep, and continued down the short passage to their own room.

She turned to face him as he closed the bedroom door behind them, switching on the centre light. 'I wish you had told me,' she said.

Stripping off his jacket as he strode past her to the wardrobe, he exclaimed. 'For heaven's sake! What difference would it make?'

'I think it might have made a lot of difference,' she said stubbornly. 'I was very upset at the time. It seemed to me like another instance of your work coming first, before—before your family.'

'*Another* instance?' His glance was hostile as he turned after hanging up his coat, his hands going to his tie and jerking it loose. 'What do you mean by that, exactly?'

'What do you think I mean?' she cried. 'I've always known that the office was the most important thing in your life——'

'Don't talk such bloody nonsense!' he snapped furiously. 'Are you trying to find excuses for your own behaviour, or what?'

'*Oh*, must you always bring everything back to that?' Catherine demanded.

'*Yes! Yes*, damn you, I must!' He stepped away from the wardrobe, his face set in an expression resembling a snarl.

She was startled into retreating from him, and he stopped dead, took a quick, hard breath and said thickly, 'I must because it's always there, it's a poison in everything we say to each other, everything we do. You know that old cliché about something that gnaws at your vitals—whatever vitals are? I know just what it means, now. Something that's constantly there, deep inside, it never goes away, no matter what you say, no matter what I do. I can't get rid of it, and it's chewing away at me, it never stops, and the worst part of it is, that it isn't going to kill me. I'm going to have to live with it. And I don't know how I'm going to do that. I don't know how I can.'

'Jason!' she whispered, appalled.

'Oh, don't look like that!' he said harshly, turning away from her as he pulled the tie from round his neck and flung it carelessly on the bed.

'You look at Jenny and Michael like that when they've scraped a knee or stubbed a toe. For God's sake don't offer me sympathy!'

Catherine stood where she was, at a loss to know what to say to him.

Jason unbuttoned his shirt and said, 'Aren't you getting ready for bed?'

'I suppose so,' she said, slowly slipping off the filmy stole she had worn in the car. She folded it into a drawer, and reached behind her for the zip of her dress as she straightened.

But Jason's hand was there already, and she jumped, seeing him regarding her sardonically in the mirror as he expertly slid the dress open down her back. 'Don't look so scared,' he said. 'I've done this hundreds of times before.'

'I know. I was just—startled. Thank you.'

He stood behind her for a moment, watching her reflection in the mirror, and she felt the muscles of her neck tense as she waited for him to move. A current of awareness pulsed between them, she felt it. Then he moved back, and out of range of the mirror. She heard him go out to the bathroom, and quickly slipped off the dress to put on a satin nightgown, pretty like all her nightwear, but quite opaque.

When Jason came back she hurried past him immediately to take her turn in the bathroom, lingering unnecessarily over creaming off her minimal makeup and combing out her hair.

But when she finally returned to the bedroom he was still up, and still wearing the dark towelling robe he had thrown on to go to the bathroom.

He was standing by the dressing table, absently turning over the silver-backed hairbrush he had given her. She stopped in the doorway, watching him warily.

He looked up, his eyes cool. 'Come in,' he said. 'I'm not going to beat you with it.'

He put the brush down as she obeyed, closing the door behind her, and thrust his hands into the pockets of the robe.

'I didn't think you were,' she said huskily. 'You're not a violent man, Jason.'

'Don't count on it,' he said softly, and her eyes widened as she felt a frisson of apprehension travel coldly up her spine.

'Do you want a divorce?' he asked suddenly.

'*No!*' Her voice was sharp with shock. Starkly, she asked, 'Do you?'

'As the injured party?' He looked at her, his eyes hooded, and then said slowly, 'So you don't want to leave me? Is it because of the children?'

Mutely she shook her head.

'What, then?' he demanded harsly. 'Won't he marry you? Don't you want to live with your lover? Or is it that he can't give you as much as I can? You say I put my work first, but I haven't heard you complain about the money it brings— you don't resent this house, your clothes, your own car, do you? Just the fact that my work, which provides all these things, takes me away from you!'

'I'm not that silly! I know you have to give time to your work—I only resent the fact that you can shove me—us—to one side while you devote yourself to it. And that day that you rang to cancel our lunch, it seemed the last straw. I didn't know that it was because of Arthur having a heart attack, you didn't explain——'

'I intended to tell you what had happened when I saw you—I didn't want to go into it over the phone. His wife was standing near when I rang you from the hospital.'

'I see. I'm sorry, but—well, it seemed that I could always be pushed aside if you had some business matter to attend to. It somehow brought matters to a head, and made me look at myself, my life—and you—us. I—went to the beach that day, remember?'

'Yes.' He looked at her with growing anger and burst out, 'For heaven's *sake*, Catherine, you're not going to tell me you slept with Thurston because I cancelled a *lunch date*!'

'No, of course not! You don't *want* to understand, do you? If you did, you might be forced to realise that there could possibly be a fault or two on your side, too. While you're playing the patriarch chastising his erring wife, you can adopt that insufferable holier-than-thou attitude, you can feel so self-righteous! And what about *you*? Do you think I believed all these years that those business trips and conferences of yours were all devoid of feminine company? I've never complained about *that*, either. But then you've always been careful not to be found out, haven't you?'

Jason looked so stunned that she knew almost immediately she was totally, unforgivably wrong. His shock was unfeigned, the pupils of his eyes dilating and his skin going suddenly pale. In an odd voice, he said, 'There's never been anything to find out, actually. My God, do you really think——' He stopped, staring at her, then she saw his face tauten in anger. 'How long have you thought that?' he asked.

Catherine shrugged. 'I don't know. Years, I suppose. I assumed——'

'Well, you assumed wrong! If you *really* thought that—didn't you care? You just went on assuming, without even saying a word to me?'

Catherine was silent, her fingers playing with the plaited satin ribbon at the waist of her nightgown.

Jason regarded her frowningly. 'You must have had some reason,' he said, 'some sort of basis for this belief of yours.'

'Not really. Just a general impression——'

'From where? Certainly not from me!'

'Those company dinners you dragged me to,' she said. 'From the innuendoes that some of the men made in conversation, I suppose. It seemed commonly known that the conferences, the trips, aren't simply matters of business.'

'Salesmen!' Jason said contemptuously. 'Young idiots, half of them, showing off their so-called sophistication. And you listened to that kind of stupid talk, and thought it applied to me?'

'It seemed that it applied to pretty well everyone. Why should you be an exception?'

His mouth twisted bitterly. 'Why indeed?' He turned abruptly away from her, his head dipping as he applied his fingers to the back of his neck, kneading it as though to relieve aching muscles. When he looked at her again, lifting his head, his hand still rested there. 'Why?' he repeated. 'My God, we've been married for eight years, and you don't know the first thing about me, do you?'

'Do you know the first thing about me?' she retorted.

'Apparently not.' He paused. 'I asked you a question before,' he said. 'You didn't answer.'

'What question?'

'Why don't you want a divorce? Why don't you want to be with your lover?'

'You—didn't give me much chance to answer.'

'Stop hedging,' he said after a moment when she stood with her eyes on the ground, her fingers twined in the satin rope. 'You are in love with him, aren't you?'

It wasn't a question that she had asked herself, and she was strangely shocked by it.

'*Aren't* you?' Jason repeated, his voice hardening.

Catherine said, 'No, I don't think so.'

'You don't *think* so?' he said sarcastically. 'Oh, great! Well, what the hell is the attraction—sex?'

'Not sex,' she said positively. 'He's attractive, of course—but that was almost incidental. No—he's gentle and kind, and I was upset, and—it just happened.'

It must have sounded lame, she knew. As an excuse it was hopeless, as a reason—inadequate in retrospect.

'Why were you upset?' Jason asked harshly.

She almost smiled, a pale, rather bitter smile. 'Chiefly because of you,' she admitted. 'Because of what's been happening to our marriage.'

'Perhaps you'd like to expand on that.'

'Oh, for heaven's sake, Jason! You must know what I mean. We've scarcely been close recently, have we?'

'You've scarcely wanted it, have you?'

'What—what do you mean?'

'You know what I mean!' he said curtly. 'You haven't exactly been welcoming my advances lately.'

'You haven't exactly been *making* any advances lately!' she accused him. 'Not for months! Until——' Until that coldly calculated lovemaking the other night.

'You'd made it abundantly clear that you weren't interested,' he said. 'How long do you think a man can go on asking when a woman is obviously reluctant? I got sick of begging for crumbs.'

'I was tired,' she said feebly. 'That's all.'

'Not too tired to take on a job. And not too tired for Russel Thurston, apparently.'

She winced, and he said, 'All right! I'm *sorry*—I can't help it. Everything comes back to that. I told you I can't just forget it. It keeps eating at me.'

She said, softly, 'Jason——' and took a step towards him, a hand going tentatively out to him.

'I told you,' he said harshly, 'don't look at me like that!'

'The way I look at Jenny and Michael when they're hurt? I look at them that way because I love them.'

His mouth went tight. 'That isn't the kind of loving I want, Catherine. Don't offer it to me.'

She stopped, her hand dropping to her side. 'What *do* you want, Jason?'

'I want a willing, passionate partner, not a wife doing her duty. Or a woman who's salving her conscience.'

'I wonder if you want me at all,' she sighed.

'Just because I take no for an answer from you, don't kid yourself that I don't want you. Sometimes it's been all I could do to stop myself from stripping you and taking you anyway, no matter how "tired" you pretended to be.'

A peculiar sensation of excitement stirred in her stomach. A smile hovered provocatively at the corner of her mouth. 'Well, darling,' she said, 'perhaps you shouldn't have taken no for an answer so easily.'

Jason's eyes narrowed on her face, and his body seemed to tense. 'Are you telling me,' he said slowly, 'that I should have raped you?'

'Not exactly,' she said. 'But—there have been times when you might have been a little more— forceful.'

He stared at her for a long moment, before a rather frightening light came into his eyes. 'Right!' he muttered grimly, and moved so suddenly that she instinctively turned, poised for flight.

He caught her before she had gone two steps, his hand jerking her arm so that she gave a small cry of pain and fear. The next moment he had swung her off her feet in his arms, and she was protesting, half laughing and half afraid, 'Jason! I didn't mean——'

'Shut up!' he snarled at her. 'You asked for this.'

He silenced her with a short, bruising kiss on her mouth, and then she was tossed on the bed and he was wrenching away the tie belt of his robe as she sat up, gasping, '*Jason*, don't!'

'I told you to keep quiet,' he muttered, throwing off the robe, and one hand pushed her back on the pillows as he came down beside her, sliding his hand from her shoulder down to the crook of her elbow and holding her still.

'Please——' she panted, trying to stave him off with one hand on his chest.

'Don't ask me to be gentle,' he said harshly, his eyes glittering. 'I don't feel gentle. I don't feel kind. I want to make love to you so thoroughly that you'll cry for mercy. I want to imprint myself on you so deeply that you won't even remember his name. I'm going to erase every memory your body has of him. I *won't* have you confusing me with *him*. I *won't*—be gentle.'

Catherine shivered, her tongue moistening dry lips as she stared back, mesmerised by the blaze in his eyes, the bitter promise in his voice. 'Well, at least,' she whispered feebly, 'can't you please turn out the light?'

His sudden laughter was totally unexpected, and

at the sound of it she went weak with relief. 'Does it bother you?' he asked, almost tolerantly.

'It's too bright.'

The amusement hadn't banished his angry passion, but it had tempered it. 'Okay,' he said. 'Don't move.'

'She watched him walk over to the switch by the door, noticing the way the muscles in his haunches tautened as he moved, the way his slight tan stopped abruptly just below waist level, and how long and sensitive his fingers looked as he reached for the switch and flicked it off.

In the darkness his image was still printed on her mind, and she watched his shadowy figure as he returned to her, and stretched her arms over her head and her toes towards the bottom of the bed, her heart thumping with a strange, pleasurable dread.

Jason sat on the side of the bed and snapped on the bedside lamp on the night table beside her. Catherine blinked up at him, caught in a seductive pose, her lips parted in anticipation.

His smile was tight. Before she could move he had swooped one hand down behind her nape and lifted her easily against him. His mouth covered hers, and he kissed her as though he expected resistance, ruthlessly.

She yielded to it for several minutes, but as his fierceness continued, she became indignant and began to struggle. Jason took no notice at first, but after a few moments he lifted his head and looked down at her mutinous face, his mouth curving in a slow smile. 'Go on,' he said softly. 'Fight me.'

Incredulously, she said, 'Do you *want* me to?'

'I want this to be nothing like it was with *him*.'

Catherine swallowed nervously. Her heart was

hammering, and there was a choking, fluttering sensation in her throat.

He tipped her head back, his fingers tugging at her hair, and his lips burned at her throat.

With an effort she protested, 'You're hurting me!'

'So?' he drawled, his voice muffled against the warmth of her skin.

Too incensed to notice that in spite of the taunting comment he had immediately released her hair and raised his head, she reacted with blind anger, fighting him in earnest, aiming for his face with her hands curled into fists.

He caught them, laughing at her, and thrust her back on the bed, flushed with temper and glaring at him helplessly.

'Let me go or I'll scream!' she promised.

'Fine.' Almost casually, he released her hands and with one swift movement tore open the front of her nightgown and pulled the ruined fabric down, sliding the straps from her arms.

She did let out an involuntarily, strangled shriek, and he said, 'Scream away, and bring my mother and the children running to see what's happening.' His grim smile held more than a hint of devilment.

Of course she couldn't do that. She caught frantically at the torn pieces of the gown, trying to cover herelf, but in seconds Jason had her wrists held securely in one hand, while the other turned her head and held it and he kissed her again. Even as she tried to escape, a hot sweet tide of desire was coursing through her body, and when his hand slipped to her breast, teasing it into rising excitement, she shuddered and moaned.

He tore his mouth from hers and bent to see what he had done, and as he closed his lips about the evidence of her desire, she pushed her fingers into his hair, holding him to her.

But even as she arched her body in ecstasy, his mouth left her, and he brought her hand down to her side, holding it there. His eyes traversed her body, as he lay with his head propped on one hand. Trying to spread her free hand across her breasts, she said faintly, 'Don't!'

Jason laughed softly. 'You absurd little prude!' He pushed away her hand, and his lips brushed her lightly, nibbling at her, keeping the dusky centres hard and erect.

His hand wandered across her midriff to her stomach. He probed the slight hollow of her navel with his thumb, then moved lower to encounter the remnant of blue satin that clung about her hips. When he made to dispense with it, she wriggled away from his grasp, and stretched out a hand to the switch of the bed lamp.

Raising his head, Jason ordered, 'Leave it.'

'No.' Her fingers touched the switch, but before she could press it his hand snaked out and captured her wrist.

She hit out at him with her other hand, and tried to reach across with it to the light. He caught that, too, and she wailed, 'Jason, *please!*'

'*No!*' he said violently. 'Not in the dark. Not this time. When you open your eyes, you're going to see *me*. No one else. Me.'

'Then I'll damn well *shut* my eyes!'

He laughed again. 'You do that, sweetheart. If you can.'

He had to release her hands to ease off the nightgown, and she made him fight for every inch of it.

Her emotions were a kaleidoscope, a crazy, brilliant mix of anger and fear and an intense, potent exhilaration. Even though Jason's fingers were hard on her wrists, his mouth almost cruelly abrasive on her skin, she knew he had no intention of really hurting her. And though she felt a thrill of satisfaction when her palm connected with his cheek before he subdued her flailing hand, or her closed fist thudded against the hard muscle of his shoulder, she took a strange pride in the way he brushed off the pain, and she revelled in the strength of his hands as he held her off, in the sweet violence of his reprisals, the punitive kisses he inflicted on her lips and on her body. Once she sank her teeth into the fleshy part of his hand, stopping when she realised that a little more pressure would break the skin and bring blood. As she paused, his eyes met hers, and she drew back, her wide gaze held by his steady grey stare.

Jason smiled and pulled her close, then his mouth exacted a punishment that made her moan and clutch at him, silently begging for the culmination of this strange combat.

But although she knew that his body, like hers, was throbbing with need, he deliberately tantalised her, withholding himself while he brought her to a pitch of pleasure that was so intense it was like pain. When she felt that she must go over the top, he stopped, letting her slide suddenly away from the peak, so that she attacked him again in frustration, sobbing, swearing at him for engaging in a cruel game.

'You closed your eyes,' he said sternly, 'Don't close your eyes.'

She tried to hit him again, helpless against his strength, and he whispered, 'Shh, shh. It's all right.' He came over her and into her in one swift, sudden movement, and immediately she went soaring straight into spasms of incredible pleasure, that went on and on until she thought she would faint with delight.

She heard Jason give a husky laugh, and he put his hand gently over her mouth, because she was shrieking softly, breathily, unable to stop. Then she felt him shudder against her and knew that they had finally reached the peak together.

CHAPTER ELEVEN

She ached slightly all over, as though she had been climbing mountains, using unaccustomed muscles. But a delicious lassitude pervaded every limb, making them heavy, soft, unwilling to move.

Jason lay on his back, his body in an attitude of arrogant abandon and utter content, his arm cradling her shoulders, and her head nestled below his chin.

Catherine felt his chest rise and fall beneath her cheek in a long, satisfied sigh. His voice slightly slurred, he asked softly, 'All right?'

'Yes.' She moved her head a little to press a kiss on the bare skin of his chest. 'You've never made love to me like that before.'

The arm holding her tensed slightly. After a moment he said, 'I did once, and you acted the next morning as though you'd been raped. How was I to know you like it rough?'

'I don't!' she protested.

'You can't tell me you didn't enjoy yourself just now. You made it very obvious.'

She knew she had, and the knowledge was embarrassing. She turned her face against him and muttered, 'Don't!'

'What's the matter? You're acting as though it's something to be ashamed of.' He shifted, moving sideways and pushing her chin up with his hand so that he could look down at her face. 'Admit that you liked it.'

'Yes, I liked it,' she said. 'But I wouldn't want

155

it to be that way every time. It—it shocks me, a bit.'

'Why? We're married. We both had a fantastic time. No one got hurt. What's shocking about that?'

'I don't know. It's just so—so basic—so violent. It's—animal.'

'We are animals. But we're intelligent beings, too. You're afraid, aren't you? Afraid of a part of your own nature. Don't be. It's there for you to use and enjoy just like every other part of your being. So you don't want it that way every time. Fine—neither do I. Lovemaking for humans isn't just instinct, it's enhanced by planning and variety—and by loving each other in so many ways that have nothing to do with sex—or very little.'

'Yes, but—like that? It felt so—uncontrollable.'

'Why should that be bad? To let go now and then—it's a human need. The time and the place chosen beforehand, there's nothing wrong about it. Look,' He held his hand up in front of her, and she winced as she saw the marks of her teeth clearly printed on his skin.

She turned her head away, closing her eyes, and he said, 'Don't be ashamed. That's proof, if you like, that no one had lost control. You might have taken a chunk out of my hand, but you didn't. You stopped before it went that far. And I haven't left bruises on you, have I?'

She shook her head, aware that, surprisingly, it was true.

'Well, stop worrying, then. There are other ways, but there's no good or bad way, no good, better, best, for that matter, just different ways for different people, different moods, different circumstances.'

He was stroking her hair, his hand softly separating the strands and letting them float back to her shoulder. Then his fingers probed lightly behind her ear, and began to caress her back, moving over her skin along the line of her spine to her waist and then returning to her nape.

Catherine nestled close to him, her lips against his chest, moving drowsily, tasting the slight saltiness of his skin.

She was almost asleep, and made no other effort to respond to his increasingly insistent caresses. She felt the stirring of his body against her bare thigh, and he shifted, lifting her higher against him, whispering, 'Shall I let you go to sleep? Do you want me to stop?'

Faintly, she shook her head. 'Don't stop,' she murmured. 'It's—nice.'

It was totally different. For a long time Jason adored her with his hands and his lips, his touch almost feather-light, sensitising her skin so that she tingled pleasantly all over. She lay totally passive, letting him move her limbs where he wanted, and turn her head to his gentle kisses—soft, tantalising kisses that barely brushed her lips, but lingered persuasively until his mouth was drawn to some irresistible part of her body.

She expected no more than this delightful plateau of dreamy bliss, but when he took possession at last, with slow, deliberate, coaxing movements, she discovered she was still capable of arousal. Her eyes opened in stunned awareness as fierce delight washed over her in wave after wave, and her arms rose above her head, her hands clenching in ecstasy and then opening like flowers against the pillow as Jason gave a low growl of triumph and spilled his seed into her.

He woke her in the morning with a kiss, and

when she opened her eyes she discovered he was already dressed, bending over the bed with one hand on the pillow beside her, the other touching her cheek. He looked handsome and refreshed and rather pleased with himself.

'Oh, what time is it?' she asked him, struggling up on the pillows.

He laughed and said, 'Time to get up. The kids have been up for ages.'

'Oh, heavens!' Catherine pushed back her tumbled hair, grabbing at his wrist to squint at his watch. 'Why didn't you wake me?'

'Because you looked too beautiful to wake. Like Venus rising from waves.'

She had slept naked, and the sheet had slipped to her waist. Hastily she pulled it up over her, her eyes indignant as he laughed again, watching.

It was ridiculous to be shy with Jason after all these years. But the look in his eyes made her terribly, deliciously aware of her nudity under the sheet, and he did have to go to work . . .

He leaned over and trailed his lips across her shoulder, then kissed her mouth lingeringly before he got up off the bed. 'I'll make some toast,' he offered, as she waited for him to go before reaching hastily for a robe to cover herself.

She had a busy day, filming a sequence on Mount Eden, in the central city, with a geologist. He walked about the grassy crater with her, and explained for the benefit of the cameras how the volcano might have erupted thousands of years before, and why it was regarded as dormant rather than completely extinct.

'Does that mean it could erupt again at any time?' she asked him.

'Theoretically, yes,' he beamed happily. 'But one

naturally hopes there would be some warning. Scientists are becoming more aware of the danger signs, and we must hope there would be adequate time to evacuate the area if there was danger of an imminent eruption.'

Inwardly Catherine sighed with relief. That sounded fairly reassuring for nervous young viewers!

They climbed up the side of the crater with some difficulty, followed by the perspiring cameramen with their equipment, and the geologist pointed out some of the other volcanic cones visible from their vantage point. 'Rangitoto, of course,' he said, 'is a very young volcano, which last erupted only a matter of three or four hundred years ago.'

'Really?' Catherine stared at the island out in the harbour. 'I didn't know that!'

'Oh, yes. When the first white men came here, there were Maoris who remembered Rangitoto's last eruption. It certainly wouldn't be safe to say that it's dead. It's only sleeping.'

The geologist had just come back from a week studying Ruapehu, a much more active volcano in the middle of the North Island, and back at the studio Catherine sat before the cameras for another fifteen minutes and asked about his experiences there. The studio library would provide film of the mountain spitting lava and rocks during one of its periodic outbursts, and the graphics department had already produced a series of diagrams showing how a volcano built up pressure and finally 'blew its top.'

'How's it coming?' Catherine asked Russel when her part was finished. 'The geologist was good, wasn't he? Very enthusiastic, and he didn't talk down, either, the way some people do when they know we're doing a children's show.'

'I think it's shaping well,' Russel agreed. 'I've learned a thing or two myself about volcanoes. Only I'm a bit worried that the kids might get bored, if it's too heavily educational. What do you think?'

'As long as we keep it fairly short, and follow with something lighthearted, I think they'll enjoy it. The graphics are very lively and colourful, and if the library comes up with some good film, it should be exciting enough for any child. We'll need some people in the mountain shots, not just fire and brimstone on its own.'

'Yes, you're right. Much more interesting for the kids if they think someone's about to be swallowed up in hot lava!'

Catherine laughed, and he looked at her sharply. 'You're different, today,' he told her.

'How?'

'I'm not really sure. Not so restrained, more free. Happier.'

She looked away from him. He was much too sensitive to her moods. It was dangerous.

'Not going to tell me?' he asked her softly.

She shook her head.

Someone brushed by them with a plastic clipboard, shouting for one of the sound men to come to the set. Russel put a hand on Catherine's arm and drew her aside, into a corner hemmed in by one of the cameras on its steel trolley.

'You know that if things had been different, we might have had a lot going for us, you and me,' he said.

'Yes. But they're not different.'

'And you're not sorry?'

'That's a loaded question.'

'I'm trying to find out what's happened to you.'

'Why?'

'Cathy,' he reproached her, 'you know why. It's not idle curiosity. I care about you—you've got to know that. Don't fence with me.'

'I'm sorry.' She was contrite. 'But I can't discuss my marriage with you, Russel.'

'Okay,' he shrugged. 'Fair enough.' He paused. 'I'm right, aren't I? You are happier?'

'You're right.'

'Good. I mean that. And I hope it lasts.'

'I intend to do everything I can to see that it does.'

It wasn't quite that simple.

Winston was discharged from the hospital, and Althea made bookings for them to fly home in another three weeks, when he was expected to be fit to stand the journey. Catherine made arrangements for the children to go to Bridie's on the days she was working, so that Althea should be spared the trouble of looking after them and her husband as well, and also to keep the house quieter for the invalid.

Jason had looked rather oddly at her when she explained the plan, but when she asked him with a faint air of challenge if he didn't approve, he merely shrugged and said, 'If you're quite satisfied . . .'

'They'll be perfectly all right with Bridie,' she said. 'They love her, and she's quite happy to do it.'

'Well and good,' he said, leaving her baffled and dissatisfied, sure that he disapproved in some way, but unable to make him admit to it.

In the night she was far from dissatisfied. Jason seemed to have unlocked a floodgate of feelings she had not known herself capable of experiencing, and he revelled in her new ability to respond with uninhibited abandon to his equally uninhibited lovemaking.

But she suffered an unpleasant shock when one night, after they had spent themselves in physical pleasure, and she lay comfortably wedged against his shoulder, he said almost casually, 'I want you to give up that job, Catherine.'

She felt herself go cold, the warmth that filled her after an invigorating session of lovemaking seeping away like melting ice.

'Why?' she asked blankly.

'*Why?* Do I have spell it out for you? You're still seeing him every other day. Do you expect me to accept that situation for ever?'

'But, Jason——'

'I was hoping you'd make the decision yourself,' he said. 'I've been waiting for you to do it, to save me having to ask. Well, you haven't. So now I'm telling you. I want you to leave.'

She sat up, steadying herself on one hand to look down at him. 'But I can't do that!' she said, appalled.

'Can't? Or won't?'

'I have a contract,' she said wildly.

'It runs out soon, doesn't it?'

'Well—technically, yes. But the programme is going well, it's popular, and we've practically been told that the option of a renewal will be taken up by the corporation.'

'But you could refuse to renew.'

'If I did that, I don't suppose I'd get another chance in a TV show. It isn't as though I'm well known enough or experienced enough to be able to pick and choose.'

'You'll still be working with Russel Thurston.'

'He's my boss and my friend,' she said slowly. 'That's all. Please, Jason, can't you accept that?'

'No, I can't. Do you know that your little affair is common knowledge?'

She went white. 'What do you mean?'

'I mean that the two of you are known to be "good friends", as they say in the trade. Someone took it on themselves to let me know, in an oblique sort of way.'

'Oh, God! I'm sorry——'

'I wasn't exactly thrilled, myself. Now do you understand why I want you to leave?'

'Yes.' Catherine chewed anxiously on her underlip. 'I—I do understand. I will think about it, I promise.'

He made an impatient sound, and reached up, his hands on her shoulders propelling her back against the pillow while he loomed over her.

'You'll think about it?' he repeated savagely. 'Five minutes ago you lay in my arms swearing you loved me.'

'I do!'

'As much as you love your "boss and friend"? I'm asking you to choose, Catherine.'

'Don't you trust me?'

'You make it rather difficult.'

Her breath sucked into her throat. 'It won't happen again, Jason, I swear it.'

'Can you swear he means nothing to you?'

About to say *yes*, she was halted by a sense of dishonesty.

Her hesitation was fatal. Jason's eyes went cold, and he let her go as though he could no longer bear to touch her. 'You can't have us both,' he said. 'Oh, I believe you when you tell me you're not sleeping with him, but I won't play King Mark to your Tristan and Isolde, thanks. The thought of the two of you exchanging yearning looks and suffering nobly sickens me.'

'We are *not* exchanging yearning looks!' she protested furiously. 'We're too busy working to do that, even if we wanted to! Which we don't!'

'No?'

'*No!* I could lie and say he means nothing to me. I'm trying to be completely honest with you, instead. He's a friend, a special friend.'

'A dear friend!'

Ignoring the sneer in his voice, she said, 'Yes, a dear friend. Do you really think I could go to bed with someone who means nothing at all to me?'

Jason was silent, his mouth tight. 'If *I* mean anything to you,' he said, 'you'll give him up.'

'I *have* given him up, in the sense that you mean,' she said. 'I haven't even seen him alone since—since then.'

'And what about him? How long do you think he'll settle for your platonic idyll?'

'You don't know him,' she said. 'You don't understand.'

'You're damned right I don't! Make your choice, Catherine. It's him or me.'

'You're being unfair,' she said quietly. 'I've already made that choice, and you know I chose you, there was no contest. Now you're asking me to choose between you and work that I love, work that means a great deal to me.'

'If it's a job you want, you can get another one.'

'There isn't another job like this one! You know that!'

He shrugged, and she said, 'You never have liked my having a job, have you? I think it's my work that you're jealous of, really. All this about my seeing Russel is just an excuse.'

'That's rubbish! If we're talking of excuses, isn't the job just an excuse to see him, if you're honest, as you claim to be? You're not an actress, you've practically no experience, and he comes along and gets you a place hostessing your own TV show, just like that!'

'Oh, what's the use!' she cried, flinging herself away from him, turning on her side. 'You won't listen, you don't want to be reasonable, you're so eaten up with jealousy you're not even capable of thinking straight!'

'Well, you know what to do about it.' he said. 'I could do with proof that you really care about me, and about our marriage.'

Catherine refused to answer, lying dry-eyed in the darkness long after he had gone to sleep beside her.

Surprisingly, Catherine found an ally in her mother-in-law. Althea had been in the kitchen, preparing a tray for Winston, while Catherine made breakfast for the children and Jason read his paper.

Afterwards, when Catherine was clearing up, Althea brought back the empty tray and said, 'Winston's going to lie in for a little while before he gets up. Is there any coffee left?'

'Sit down,' Catherine said automatically. 'I'll get you some.'

'Thank you, dear.'

Catherine, feeling the need of a mild stimulant, poured a cup for herself as well and joined the other woman at the table.

'Have you and Jason been arguing?' Althea enquired.

'What makes you think so?' Catherine asked cautiously, her defense mechanisms rushing into play.

'I know my son, dear. When he glowers like that there's trouble brewing for someone. He always used to look exactly that way when he didn't get his own way as a child.'

'I've never been able to imagine Jason as a child,' Catherine confessed.

Unexpectedly, Althea laughed. 'Oh, he was one—for a very short time, I'm afraid. Winston always insisted on him being a little man, and he was mature by the time he was sixteen, I think. You don't have them for very long.' She paused. 'You seemed very young for him, when I met you. I thought that——'

'That it might not work out for us?'

Althea nodded. 'I was afraid that he was seeking his own youth in you—the youth that he never really had. Winston was always so keen for him to assume his responsibilities—and when Jason went into the business it didn't work out. They clashed terribly. It was much better when Jason followed his own bent and struck out independently. Of course there were rows. I had tried to warn Winston, but he's a very stubborn man—Jason has inherited that, too, you'll know. And I didn't ever have a great deal of say in his upbringing. Winston always said he'd take care of the boys, and leave the girls to me. Only there never were any girls, of course, and by the time we realised there weren't going to be any, Jason was very much his daddy's boy.'

'I'm sorry,' Catherine murmured.

'Oh, well.' Althea sipped at her coffee, holding the cup in both her long, veined hands. 'It's all water under the bridge now. I try to compensate with Jason's—your—children, Catherine. Do you mind very much?'

'No.' She had minded terribly, especially when she had been younger and very unsure of herself. Now, with a glimmering of understanding, she felt able to view Althea's interference a little more tolerantly.

Althea smiled, a little sadly. 'I expect you do, really. Anyway, we'll be gone in a couple of weeks, now, and you'll have them all to yourself again.'

'They'll miss you,' Catherine told her.

'I daresay they will, for a little while. Will you let us have them again, some time?'

'Yes, of course, they loved staying with you.'

'Will they keep going to your friend while you're working?'

'I don't know. Bridie won't let me give her money. I may need to get a regular babysitter.'

Althea said nothing, and Catherine said rather defensively, 'Jason wants me to stop working. There would be no need to bother with someone to look after them, if I do.'

'Are you going to?'

'Probably.' Catherine stirred her coffee unnecessarily, brooding.

'I shouldn't, if I were you,' said Althea.

Catherine stared in astonishment. She had been quite certain that Althea disapproved of her working. 'You wouldn't?' she echoed blankly. 'But I thought—I was sure you would agree with Jason.'

'I admit I didn't like the idea at first,' said Althea. 'But I've been thinking, since Winston had this heart attack. I suppose I'm a very selfish woman, but once I got over the initial shock, and when we were told that he wasn't going to die, all sorts of strange thoughts occurred to me. At least, they were strange to me.'

She paused abruptly, as though embarrassed, and Catherine queried, 'What kind of thoughts?'

'Well,' Althea said slowly, 'I thought—I've devoted my life to this man, to looking after his home, his health, his interests, his son, even. That's how I always think of Jason, you know, as Winston's son. Odd, I suppose, but then Winston is such a very forceful man, he—stamps ownership on everything. Including me. I was quite a nice-looking girl, you know, when we got married, and for a long time afterwards, because Winston liked me to look good, he never stinted me for clothes, make-up, anything like that—but I would never have dared to stray. There were chances, but—well, I never took them. Anyway, I thought, here I am, and I've submerged myself in this man, what do I have of my own, what would I do if he wasn't here for me to care for, listen to, pick up after? What will I do if I'm left on my own? I would exist on Winston's money, make myself a sort of walking, talking monument to his memory.'

Catherine stared at her, fascinated, appalled. Althea put down her cup and said, 'Don't get me wrong, my dear. I love Winston—I'm very fond of him. And I know that he thinks the world of me. But, you see, I've allowed myself to become an extension of him. I have no real existence of my own. Even our friends—I think they've all been business acquaintances of Winston's, to begin with. They're his friends, really; he chose the men, and I had to get along with the women. I had one really close girl friend before we were married, but she and Winston didn't click, somehow. I never see her now, not for years and years. Sometimes I wonder where she is, what she's doing. We'd known each other since we were five years old.'

'That's very sad.'

'Yes, I suppose it is. One stops minding as one gets older. I see that shocks you, too. I've talked too much.'

'No, you haven't. I'm glad you felt able to talk to me.'

'Well, I hope it made some sense. You've changed, you know,' Althea told her, 'I've never felt able to really talk to you before. The generation gap, I suppose. You've always seemed so very young and—brittle, somehow, as though a wrong word could shatter you. You're much more resilient, now, more self-assured. Perhaps it's that job.'

'It's given me a lot of confidence in myself that I didn't have before,' said Catherine. 'I don't want to give it up.'

'Then don't. A few hours a week without you won't harm the children; in fact, it might be good for them. They're not babies. And Jason is growing too much like his father. They have admirable qualities, both of them, but they're much too fond of laying down the law and expecting others to toe the line. Stand up to him.'

'Perhaps I will.' But of course the situation was much more complex than Althea was aware of. Exchanging confidences with her was too novel an experience for Catherine to go any further. But Althea's support did somehow bring a new dimension to bear. She had been racked with guilt and indecision ever since Jason had given his ultimatum. Shouldn't she be ready and willing to give up her job to save their marriage, to prove to him that she did really love him? She had accused him of putting his work before her—wasn't she now guilty of doing the same?

And yet it seemed unfair. She loved her job, it was doing no one any harm, she was still doing her duty as his wife, and the mother of his children. Should she bow to an unreasonable demand, just because he made it, as her husband?

A Victorian wife, of course, would have had no hesitation, and indeed no choice. But times had moved on since then. Didn't a woman have an equal right to self-fulfilment outside the home as well as within it?

When Jason arrived home that night, he gave her a hard, questioning look. Catherine knew that when they were alone in the privacy of their own room, he would be waiting for her answer. She wasn't ready yet to give it.

CHAPTER TWELVE

THE next day was Saturday. The children wanted to go the zoo, and Catherine thought it would be a good idea on several counts. It would leave the house quiet for Winston, give the children some time with both their mother and father, and ease the illogical guilt she felt about letting someone else care for them on the afternoons that she was working. She had vague hopes, too, that a day out with the children might help to bring herself and Jason closer together, creating a climate of understanding.

The outing began promisingly enough. They started by visiting the kiwi house near the main gate, and in the eerie blue dimness, the children pressed their noses against the glass to watch the nocturnal birds rooting about in the artificial bush environment that had been provided for them, eagerly pointing and whispering when they spotted one.

But before they had finished viewing the remainder of the bird section, Michael was restlessly demanding to visit the tigers and lions, while Jenny wanted to see the elephant. Sensing a quarrel brewing, Catherine moved from Jason's side to hold the children's hands, one on either side of her, and exerted herself to keep them interested while they strolled past the peacocks and she steered them towards the aquarium and the nearby elephant enclosure.

Fortunately there was a baby elephant in the excercise yard, and watching it feed was so fascinating that for a time Michael was quite content to stay there, until Jenny too was ready to see the lions.

Further on were cages of monkeys, and Jason was persuaded to accede to the children's request to buy some peanuts to give them.

'Don't use them all at once,' he warned them. 'Save some for later.'

They had a picnic lunch on one of the lawns, admiring the graceful attitudes of pink flamingoes posing by a stream, and then the children reminded them that they had still to see the hippos, and that the seals would be fed later in the afternoon.

The day had become hot, and the pavements seemed hard to Catherine's feet. The children would not think of leaving without seeing everything, but Jenny's dragging feet and Michael's increasingly red face told their own tale.

Ice creams all round might be a good idea, Catherine thought, as she sank down for a few restful moments on a low stone wall, watching the children a few yards away talking to some more monkeys.

Jason came and propped himself beside her with his arms folded across his chest. 'They seem to be enjoying themselves,' he remarked. 'And they're less fractious than they've seemed to be lately. I wonder if Bridie tends to give in to them too much, or if they just miss not having you about.'

His reasoning was very transparent, she thought angrily. Giving herself a moment or two to quell the anger, she replied evenly, 'It isn't Bridie's fault, or mine. Haven't you noticed how Althea and Winston give in all the time to Jenny, and harp on Michael's being a big boy? He sees it as favouritism. He's jealous, and Jenny trades on the fact of being younger, and being able to get her own way with your parents.'

She wasn't sure if he had taken in what she said, because his eyes were on the children, who were conducting a tug-of-war over the remaining peanuts in their paper bag, Michael holding the neck of the bag with an expression of grim determination, while Jenny tugged at it and whined disagreeably.

'Famous last words,' Jason murmured. 'Hadn't you better do something about that before it develops into a full-scale war?'

Her patience suddenly snapping, she said, 'Do something about it yourself! They're your children as well as mine.'

He cast her such an incredulous look that she almost laughed, but then he went over to the children.

She didn't hear what he said, but the tone of his voice stopped the tug-of-war immediately, and then he went down on his haunches and spoke to them until Michael handed over the bag of peanuts to him, allowing him to divide the remaining nuts between them.

Jason took charge from then on. He bought cool drinks and ice creams, made the children slow their pace a little, and a couple of times found Catherine a seat in the shade while he strolled nearby in the sun with Jenny and Michael as they studied the animals.

Only when, after seeing the seals fed, Jenny demanded the toilet, did he turn to Catherine, saying dryly, 'Your department, I think.'

The rest of the day was certainly less stressful, and yet Catherine arrived home feeling vaguely resentful and irritated.

Jason had bought some fried chicken for their evening meal, a treat the children always enjoyed. They ate with gusto, pausing between mouthfuls to regale Winston and Althea with details of their day, so that the result was a non-stop commentary to which their grandparents listened with flatteringly close attention.

Under cover of the conversation, Jason said to Catherine, 'Are you tired?'

She shook her head. Her feet ached a little and she was conscious of heat and a slight stinging where her bared shoulders had got sunburned, but she was not particularly weary. 'I'm all right,' she said. 'Why?'

'You seem very—quiet.'

'The children are doing enough talking for all of us, surely.'

He smiled briefly, looking at them, but then his eyes returned sceptically to her.

When the children had finally gone off to bed, Althea said, 'Winston and I have only one weekend left here. Why don't you two take the opportunity of a couple of days away, and let us look after the children?'

'We couldn't——' Catherine started to say, but Jason overrode her protest.

'We'd like that very much,' he said. 'If you're sure you could cope.'

'Of course,' Althea said almost breezily. 'We had them for nearly three months back home.'

'Yes,' Catherine intervened swiftly, 'but that was before Winston's illness.'

'I'm fine now,' Winston assured her. 'We'd enjoy having the youngsters to ourselves for a day or two. You go away with your husband and have a good time.'

'It isn't long since we had a week away,'

Catherine objected. Somehow she felt crowded, almost panicky at this unexpected gesture, and their determination to make her take advantage of it.

'Darling,' Jason said smoothly, 'if you keep putting up obstacles, my parents will think you don't want to go away with me.'

She swivelled to look at him, suddenly assailed by a suspicion that he had engineered this whole thing. But there was a warning in his eyes. He knew she didn't want Althea and Winston to guess that all was not well with their relationship.

Reluctantly, she conceded, but the panic inexplicably increased. 'Yes, well, if you're sure you don't mind,' she said. 'It's very generous of you.'

Later she said to Jason, 'Did you ask your mother to make that offer?'

'What offer?'

'You're not stupid, Jason!' she snapped. 'You know perfectly well what I mean! Was it your idea, this weekend away while Althea and Winston mind the kids?'

'I mentioned that I'd like some time alone with my wife.'

'What have you been telling her?'

'Nothing.' His glance was impatient. 'Stop trying to pick a fight.'

'I'm not doing anything of the kind!'

'Yes, you are. Your nose has been out of joint ever since I took up your challenge this afternoon and took charge of *my* kids. You wanted me to come a cropper, and I didn't.'

'That's a ridiculous thing to say!'

'Is it? Then why have you been looking daggers at me ever since?'

'You're imagining things,' Catherine said coldly.

He laughed. 'No, I'm not. I know you pretty well. You know, you don't play fair.'

'What do you mean?'

She was already in bed, propped on the pillows with a book in her hand. Jason had pulled off his shirt and was tugging at the buckle on his belt. He had his back half turned to her as he stepped out of his trousers and pulled on a robe.

'What do you mean?' Catherine repeated impatiently.

He stood doing up the tie belt, his eyes assessing her. 'I guess I mean that you started our marriage happily prepared to abide by certain rules of the game, certain assumptions that we both tacitly accepted. Now you want to change the rules.'

She frowned, and he said, tugging at the knot he had made, 'Well, okay, fine. But you might have warned me you wanted to change them, before you started blaming me for playing by the old rules. If you're going to start making up new ones unilaterally, you should at least tell me what they are. Right now I'm playing in the dark, trying to guess the shots.'

'I don't know what you're talking about!' she said crossly. 'I'm not calling any shots.'

'Yes, you are, sweetheart. You always have. Think about it. We'll talk about it next weekend.'

Jason went off to the bathroom, and Catherine sat looking at her book and not taking in a word of print. What had he meant by all that? What was she supposed to think about? She shifted restlessly, dug her elbow into the pillow and slammed the book shut. The more she contemplated the weekend, the more uneasy she felt. Jason, she was afraid, was determined on some kind of showdown.

He took her north again, but this time they didn't make for the Bay of Islands, but for the Hokianga, the long, enclosed harbour on the other side of the Northland isthmus. Here the tranquil water was soft as satin, and as smooth, and the gentle hills dipped their feet into its reflecting mirror, and fishing boats and occasional ferries cut transient paths across its surface.

Jason had obtained a small cottage overlooking the water, in the little town of Rawene, where the main street humped itself to the harbour's edge like an asphalt caterpillar, and some of the shops were built on stilts sunk into the water. One of its earliest houses, converted to a museum of history, still sat on a small rise overlooking the harbour, surrounded by great shade trees which added to its air of graciousness. But of the area's busy days as a thriving centre of timbermilling, boatbuilding and water transport, little remained.

Catherine pretended an interest in the history of the district, but Jason soon called her bluff. He produced a booklet which gave her more information than she had ever wanted, and asked her which historical sites she wanted to see. They visited Clendon House and duly admired the Victorian relics that filled it, strolled about the harbour's edge, and stared at the peculiar shape of the old wooden store which honoured the triangular shape of the road junction at the foot of the main street by fitting into it. They even ferried across the harbour to Kohukohu and back again, watching the changing light gradually shade the hills and the harbour into different blends of grey, blue, green and subtle silver.

Slowly, Catherine felt the tensions of the last weeks and months begin to ease from her soul. The quietness of the hills, the tranquillity of the great spreading sheet of water, the sleepy air of the little town, had soothed her into a state bordering on serenity.

Jason, too, seemed more relaxed, his gaze less penetrating when he looked at her, the line of his mouth less grim. On Friday night they had arrived late, and had a quick supper and fallen into bed to sleep. But Saturday evening they ate fresh fish bought at the harbourside, and Jason produced a bottle of white wine to complement it. Then they sat on the wooden steps outside overlooking the water, and watched the dying sun throw ribbons of flame across it, and the first stars sprinkle themselves across the darkening sky.

Jason got up and came back with two glasses filled with the remainder of the wine they had had at dinner. Catherine took one when he handed it to her, and he sat down again, leaning his back against the door jamb where he could watch her face.

'Okay,' he said. 'Time to talk.'

Catherine stiffened. Lightly, she said, 'You sound like a Nazi interrogator.'

He smiled, but his glance was wary. 'Don't go all resentful on me again,' he said. 'I'm willing to try and understand, believe me.'

'Understand what?' She was wary, now, too.

'You. Myself. Don't you think it's time we really talked?'

'You mean you have time?' she asked. She heard the sarcasm in her own voice, and bit her lip.

Jason turned the glass in his hand, watching the liquid swirl, shining in the dimness. 'Right, we'll start there,' he said. 'You think you're second best to my work. I need my work. It isn't just a job, something I do because I have to earn a living. It's challenging and interesting and I'm good at it, and that gives me a kick, I suppose, some sort of ego boost. But I'd give it up tomorrow if I thought it was damaging my relationship with you. It hasn't ever been first with me since I met you. I've always been ambitious, and you know I needed to work damned hard to get where I have. I thought my success at the job was one of the things that attracted you to me in the first place. I find it absorbing, but I never meant to exclude you. I've needed to know that you were there in the centre of my life. Otherwise none of it has any meaning.'

'You've never told me this before,' she said shakily. 'Never anything like it.'

'I thought you knew without being told.'

She shook her head, and said, 'We haven't always communicated very well, have we? You've been caught up in your job, and I've been concentrating so hard on the children—when did we stop talking to each other?'

'We communicated in other ways——'

'Yes, and I know you thought that it was enough. But it isn't, Jason. And eventually that broke down, too, didn't it? Sex and the children are strong bonds, but not strong enough.'

'I know. That's why I wanted this time together. To talk.'

'Yes. Jason, I know you think my job is a sort of stop-gap, like the other things I tried and tired of. But it isn't. This is important to me. For the first time in my life, I feel like a real person in my own right, someone who's doing something productive and creative in more than just a biological sense.'

'You mean you see motherhood as a purely biological function? But surely it's much more than that? You've always been a tremendously conscientious mother. You read everything you could lay your hands on about child care, you even chose Playcentre instead of kindergarten because of the greater parent involvement.'

'*You* didn't care to be too involved, I remember.'

'You're thinking of those Fathers' Days they had. Okay, I admit I felt useless when Michael asked me to help him make a truck like the one his friend's dad made. I've never been good with carpentry. I'll lay you odds his friend's father was a carpenter by trade. And I'm not very good at imagining I'm a fireman, either. I didn't mind going along, but I was always deathly afraid that Michael would be horribly embarrassed by his father's inadequacies.'

'Jason!' Catherine gaped at him over her glass, scarcely able to credit the selfconscious admission. 'Did you feel you had to compete with the other fathers? But that's ridiculous! All Michael and Jenny ever wanted was for you to just be there!'

'Rot. They wanted to show me off. That's what fathers are for at that age. Or maybe——'

'Maybe what?'

He shrugged. 'Maybe—oh, this is a little twisted, I guess. But, you see, *my* father was very competitive, and he bred me the same way. I could never quite come up to his standard. I suppose I was really afraid that my son would find me wanting, too.'

While she was still reeling with surprise, he added, 'And then, you were so very efficient as a parent, they didn't really seem to need two of us.'

'But of course they need two of us!'

'Oh, yes. Your books and courses stressed that, I know. But I was pretty much a figurehead father, wasn't I, Catherine? Something the kids should have, like clean clothes and plenty of fresh vegetables and bedtime stories. You made it pretty clear that you were the child expert in our home. I was handy for outings and presents and playing games, and occasionally I could help bath them or change a nappy if you were sick or extra busy. But you made all the decisions, you were the one who determined how they were to be brought up. I'm not complaining. You did a good job, I approved of the way you handled things. No doubt I was guilty, too, of a certain laziness. It was convenient to leave it all to you, it let me out of most of the more unpleasant aspects of parenting. Only now you're beginning to want me to take on my share. Fair enough, but don't try and make me feel guilty for letting you do it yourself for so long. Because it seems to me that was exactly the way you wanted it.'

Catherine got up and walked a little way along the uneven path with a weedy, overgrown garden bordering it. Her first instinct was to defend herself, accuse him of misrepresenting the facts. But, forcing herself to try and look at his view objectively, she had to admit that there was a lot of truth in it. She had taken a pride in being a good mother, it had been important to her. And she had, perhaps, guarded her domain a little too jealously.

'You may be right,' she admitted. 'I didn't realise that I was pushing you out, but the house—the children—they were the things that gave me a feeling of worth, you see. They were my—areas of competence. I didn't want to share them with anyone—even you. And I think I wanted to show you that I could shine, too, in my own little sphere. You were always so assured, so successful. And you never really took me seriously.'

'I can't buy that,' Jason said swiftly. 'I took you seriously enough to marry you!'

'Yes, why?' she asked suddenly, turning to look at him fully. 'Did you think I was young enough to be malleable, that you'd be able to mould me to your requirements? I did try, you know. I tried for a long time, but I know that as a business wife, I've failed you.'

'I married you because I was madly in love with you. And I'd always made straight for what I wanted, and got it. I know it was unfair, that you were too young to know anything about loving, about marriage, especially marriage to an unscrupulous egoist like me. You were too inexperienced to know what you really wanted, or to stand up to me. By the time I woke up to the fact that there's more to love than taking what one loves, we'd been married for some time. I tried to make it up to you, give you everything you could possibly need or want, even restrained my need of you ... And I lived in dread that one day you'd really fall in love, and then you'd realise what you'd been missing, and leave me. You don't know what I've gone through these last few months. I thought, this is it. This is where she finds out what I've done to her. This is the end.'

'But it wasn't.'

'No. I've got a reprieve. You said you don't love him. So I've got another chance to make it me, after all. And, Catherine, I'm trying. I'm trying so hard.'

'It *is* you, Jason,' she said softly. 'Don't you know I love you?' She stared at him in the rapidly growing gloom, his hand curved about his glass, his face brooding.

'You want me to give up working,' she said. 'You want that as proof that I love you.'

'Is it so hard?'

'Yes. You said you'd give yours up tomorrow,

but that's hypothetical, isn't it? And we both know it. It would be an absurd, ridiculous and pointless gesture. Supposing I asked you to do it, anyway? Would you find it easy?'

He moved impatiently. 'Do you remember all the times you've made the children your excuse not to attend a business dinner or a conference with me? It compares oddly with your readiness to let my mother or Bridie or even a hired sitter care for them while you go to work. Remember the times you said you were too tired to dress up for some office party? I've seen how you've enjoyed dressing carefully for your television appearances. You accused me of being jealous of your job. Well, I am. Even before I knew about you and Russel Thurston, I was scared that you'd meet someone—someone you wouldn't mind dressing up for, someone you'd be proud to go into company with.'

'I'm sorry,' she stammered. 'I just—came to resent being a sort of buttonhole.'

'What?'

'Being taken along as a decorative addition,' she said. 'You know, "and wife" as specified on the invitations. I had no real purpose at those functions, except as some sort of adjunct to you. Looking after the children was just an excuse. I hardly realised it myself.'

He frowned. 'I never thought of you as a decorative addition. I'm proud of you, and I wanted your company, that's all. But I suppose— you thought I wanted you along for reasons that had nothing to do with what *you* would like to do. Okay, I can see that.'

'Can you? And can you see why I'm reluctant to give up my job?' She saw him stiffen, and said swiftly, 'I will, Jason, if you insist. But I wish you

wouldn't. Because I know how it will be. I'll resent
being made to do it, though I'd try not to. I
wouldn't be able to help it. I know you don't want
me to change, you want to put me in a little gilded
cage, always the child bride you married. I'm
sorry, but I can't be that any more. I'm a grown
woman. I need to feel like one. I do want to
change the rules. Adults don't need them.'

He stood up, first putting his glass down on the
step. Then he came over and took her and put it
down, too. He placed his hands on either side of
her face and turned it up to him.

'You ask a lot,' he said.

'I know.' She stared back at him, willing him to
understand. 'Please trust me, Jason. It isn't the
man, it's the job. Just the job.'

'I'm desperately afraid of losing you,' he told
her, his thumbs moving against her skin. 'I
probably always will be. But I don't want a good,
dutiful little wife being a martyr for my sake. I
hate the thought of you seeing him—I hate it. But
I'm trying to examine my own motives, my
feelings.'

'It's all right,' she said, touching his sleeve. 'I'll
give it up.' She couldn't stand the pain in his voice,
but she couldn't hide the defeat in hers.

Jason's hands tightened about her face, and he
kissed her fiercely. But as his mouth left hers, he
said, almost violently, 'No!'

He stared down at her in the growing darkness,
and said, 'No. You said you'd resent it, in time.
And you'd be right. I don't have the right to exact
sacrifices from you ... I only have the right to
love you. And I do. I love you and I have to trust
you. I've seen you changing, growing, and it scares
me. But I can't stop you, I don't really want to, I
want it to happen for you, just the way you would

like. I can't cage your heart, and that's what I want, the essential you that stays Catherine, no matter what changes age and experience bring. There will always be something there that is you, Catherine, the woman I love. I'll always love you, old rules or new. That can't change.'

'You're changing, too, Jason. And surely a marriage that doesn't change can't remain vital, can't last, it can only disintegrate or gradually wither away. Ours won't. We won't let it. Am I making sense?'

'Marvellous sense, my darling. We'll give it lots of room to grow, and we'll nurture it with tolerance and water it with love. And speaking of love—see that moon over the water?'

Catherine turned her head and saw the huge orange globe hanging just over the dark shadows of the hilltops.

'I see it,' she said. 'It's a lovers' moon.'

'And we're lovers, aren't we?'

'An old married couple like us?'

'We're not old. But when we are, we'll still be lovers. I'll see to it.'

Catherine giggled. 'And here I was just thinking what a liberated male you'd turned out to be! What do you mean——' she went on with mock indignation '—you'll see to it?'

'I'll show you,' Jason said calmly, and picked her up in his arms. She gasped and laughed as he strode up the steps and slammed the door with his foot.

'Where's the damned bed?' he growled into the darkness, and she smothered her laughter against his throat and said, 'I should think a macho male like you could find it by instinct.'

A moment later she found herself thrown on to eiderdown softness.

'How's that for instinct?' he asked in her ear as his hard body came against her. 'And how's this?' His mouth found hers unerringly, and she had only time to murmur against his lips, 'Pretty damn good,' before words became superfluous, and laughter was submerged in a delicious, sweeping tide of passion.

The moon had paled and was sailing high in the sky by the time the passion had spent itself and they lay twined together with the tumbled eiderdown, their fingers gently exploring again the terrain that had been intimately traversed already.

When Jason moved the quilt, she said protestingly, 'Hey! You can't have it all!'

'I don't want it all. I want to see you in the moonlight. You're incredibly beautiful. Are you cold?'

'No,' she admitted. She put her hands up teasingly to close his eyes with her fingers.

'Don't you like me looking?' he asked, obediently allowing her to stop him.

Catherine removed her fingers to slide her hands about his neck, and bring him close to her, his cheek against hers, his body coming back to her side. 'It's all right,' she said. 'But I'd rather touch. Do you mind?'

He kissed her cheek. 'Whatever you say, ma'am.'

She laughed. 'You've changed your tune! Whatever happened to the masterful type who just threw me down here and had his way with me?'

'Do you miss him?'

'Mm—I don't know. This one's rather sweet.'

'Sweet!'

'Very sweet,' Catherine said firmly.

'I'd say that's a surefire way to bring your masterful lover back—if you want him?'

'I want them both,' she said. 'And all the others you have hidden away in there. I've met one or two already. You never told me you were a multiple personality.'

'Shh! That's a secret between me and my psychiatrist.'

She laughed. She was still laughing when he kissed her, his own shoulders shaking as their open, laughing mouths met.

Another one, she thought. There are so many ways. And all of them good. And we still have so much to explore together, so much to discover about each other and about ourselves.

The years stretched ahead gloriously, full of promise, the promise of change and growth, sustained by a changing and growing love.

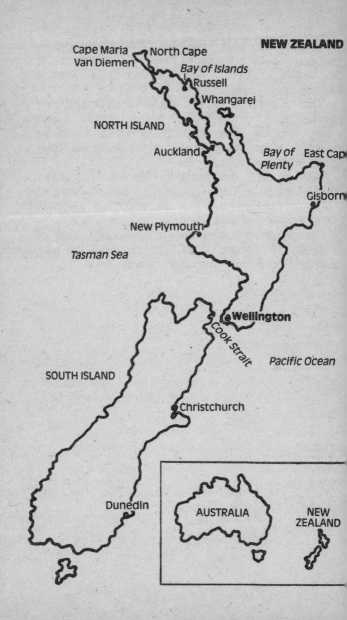

Take these 4 best-selling novels FREE

Marriage, home, kids— was that her life?

Catherine had married Jason Clyde when she was only eighteen—scarcely more than a child. Jason had been handsome, successful, older, and he had swept her off her feet.

Now, eight years later, she felt herself becoming restless. She still loved Jason and treasured her two children, but she began to wonder if her life could include more than being someone's wife, someone's mother.

Then she met Russel Thurston, a handsome, sympathetic TV producer, who showed her a world apart from Jason.

Could her marriage survive the change in her?

DAPHNE CLAIR is a New Zealand author popular in both the Harlequin Romance and Presents series. Readers delight in the bold, innovative plots characteristic of her books.

 Harlequin is romance

...and you can never have too much romance.

ISBN 0-373-10687-4

Thirty-five Years of Excellence

10687

PRINTED IN U.S.A.

0

65373 00195